Praise For

THE BRONZE DAGGER & THE STOLEN JEWELS

Dr. Sontag captures the ancient Mesopotamian culture in a captivating tale of a young boy's survival. Armed with his lucky dagger, Sam sets out on an adventure where he encounters numerous challenges and foibles, leading him to a lesson in forgiveness. A great read!

~Dr. Donna Lewis, Educator
Assistant Superintendent

The book pulls you into history through well-written narrative. By the end of the tale you come away with not only an interest in the characters and storyline, but more knowledge about the time of the Babylonians.

~Rick Crawford, Former Principal
Author of *Stink Bomb*, and *Ricky Robinson Braveheart*

Praise For

THE WHITCOMB DISCOVERIES

This book [California Trail Discovered] contains History, Literature, Geography, and STEAM all in one! As a home-school teacher, I appreciated how all of these subjects were woven together in one place, and as an avid reader, I loved that the lessons did not make the storyline feel awkward or forced. Pacing in this story was excellent, and character development

was not sacrificed on behalf of action, as there was an abundance of both. I loved reading Daniel's story; I highly recommend it!
~Rachel Summey, Homeschooling Mom
Richardson, Texas

*A*dventurous and historical, this delightful story is a page turner and engaging, providing a vivid reminder of the challenges of the California Gold Rush era as the miners and settlers clashed with the Native Americans over resources. Daniel's character was particularly enjoyable. He is human, kindhearted, and imperfect in a wonderful way. He is introspective as he works through an internal struggle with past misdeeds and life decisions.
~Kim Hamm, Middle School Teacher
California

*Y*osemite Trail Discovered reveals much about the California Gold Rush era, Westward expansion, slavery, U.S. treatment of Native Americans, growth of California towns, and more. Best of all, it provides a gripping story. This YA historical novel will be an entertaining goldmine for young people, especially those learning about the origins of California as a state. Teachers will find it a useful tool.
~Colleen Peterson, PhD
Author of Lucia's Renaissance

The
Bronze
Dagger

The Ancient Elements Series
Volume 1

The
Bronze
Dagger
&
The Stolen Jewels

MARIE SONTAG

WordCrafts Press

The Bronze Dagger & the Stolen Jewels is a work of fiction. The author has endeavored to be as accurate as possible with regard to the times and places in which the events of this novel are set. Still, this is a novel, and as such all references to persons, places, and events are fictitious or are used fictitiously.

The Bronze Dagger & the Stolen Jewels
Copyright © 2013
Marie Sontag, PhD

ISBN: 978-1-957344-69-0

Cover design by Farhan Harits.
Map design by Libby B. Hall.

Published by WordCrafts Press
Cody, Wyoming 82414
www.wordcrafts.net

To my grandchildren, Noah and Claire.
You two make up the best story of my life!

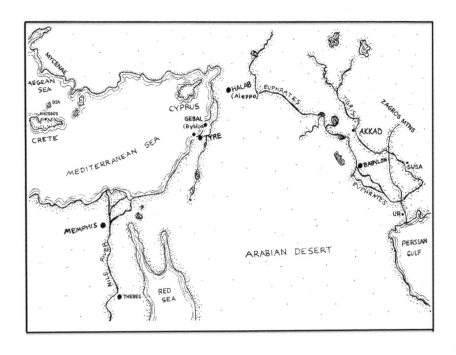

CHAPTER 1

THE LUCKY DAGGER

In the 27th year of the reign of Hammurabi, King of Babylon
1765 BC, Zagros Mountains to Susa

Exhausted from his moon-lit trek down the mountainside, Sam stumbled into Susa just before dawn. His grumbling stomach and the scent of fresh bread led him to the back of a bakery shop. Arriving before it opened, Sam slumped behind a group of tall jars and dozed off.

"You! What are you doing behind our shop? Shoo!" someone shouted.

Disoriented from last night's ordeal and his lack of sleep, Sam found it hard to focus. After rubbing his eyes, the form of a bushy-haired boy took shape.

"Are you deaf? You must leave at once!" With raised fists, the boy stepped closer.

Not finding his walking stick, Sam scrambled to his knees. He bumped into one of the large clay jars, almost knocking it over.

"Please." Sam's voice came soft and small as he eyed a bag of bread slung over the boy's shoulder. "Could you spare a small piece of bread?" When was the last time he'd eaten? He'd walked all night from the Zagros foothills to the city of Susa.

His stomach growled as loud as two wolves ready to pounce upon their prey.

"Ack! A beggar, eh? By the gods!" The boy wagged his finger. "My parents don't approve of strays. You'd better leave before they see you. They might have you arrested."

In the dim light of the early morning, Sam peered more closely into the boy's large brown eyes. The lad looked about his own age, perhaps thirteen or fourteen. "I'm not a beggar," Sam said. Grabbing his walking stick, he stood and limped closer. "A cheetah attacked me last night while I watched my sheep, so I came to the city to find my uncle. Surely, you could spare a small morsel of bread."

The tightness in the boy's face slackened. He began to remove a loaf of bread from his bag but stopped when tiny chirps sounded nearby. "Gilgamesh, is that you?"

Sam followed the boy as he searched behind the jars. Finally, the young man stopped in front of the tallest jar. On the ground lay a small brown and white bird.

Sam leaned on his stick and took a closer look. "There's a tiny gash on his belly."

The bakery boy crouched and stroked the small bird's beak. "Gilgamesh, what happened to you?"

Sam eyed the bag of bread still dangling from the boy's shoulder. His empty stomach growled again. If he treated the bird, maybe he'd get food in return. He glanced up at the boy. "Once while shepherding my sheep, a wolf snatched one of my lambs. I chased the wolf off, but the wolf left severe bite marks on the lamb's back. I treated wounds with an ointment I discovered, and they healed quickly. If we take Gilgamesh inside, maybe I can help him too."

The boy nodded, gently scooped up the injured bird, and led Sam through a side door of the bakery shop.

"Just as my parents don't approve of strays, they also don't

ooy laid the bird on a low wooden table.
. near the marshes a week ago when a fox
. I scared the fox away. When I saw the bird
.. ny, I brought it home. My parents don't know I've
been taking care of it, and I hope to keep it that way. By the
way, I'm Enlil."

Sam pulled out a bronze knife from beneath his tunic.

Enlil stepped back.

"Don't worry," Sam said. "I'm just going to put some medicine
on Gilgamesh's wing." Sam withdrew a brownish-green nut
from his leather pouch and cut a hole in it. He then scraped
a gummy green substance out of the nut and spread it on the
bird's wing. After limping outside and searching the weeds, he
returned with an insect and placed it into Gilgamesh's beak.

"That might make him feel a little better." Sam returned the
gall nut to his pouch. "Enlil, I'm glad to meet you and Gilgamesh. My name's Samsuluna. You can call me Sam."

Enlil removed a round loaf from his cotton sack. "Thanks
for helping me with Gilgamesh." He motioned for Sam to sit
on a nearby mat next to the table. He tore off a large chunk of
bread and handed it to Sam.

"So, Sam, you were attacked by a cheetah last night?"

Sam chewed his bread and swallowed. "Yes. My sheep scat-
tered after the attack, so I walked all night to reach the city.
Since my parents are dead, now I'm looking for my uncle."
After finishing his bread, he glanced around the room to avoid
Enlil's gaze.

"This used to be my older brother's bedroom," Enlil said. "He
got married last year and moved to Babylon."

Sam's chin trembled. "Do you miss your brother?" His voice
came low and soft.

"Yes, I miss him something awful. Whenever I feel lone-
some, I come into his room and think about all the good times

we had together. My parents never come in here. They say it will bring bad luck if they do, and then something bad might happen to Lurs. That's my brother, Lurs. He serves in one of King Hammurabi's top battalions in Babylon. Now that Lurs is gone, I have twice the chores I used to have." Enlil widened his eyes. "May the gods have mercy. I'm late for my deliveries! Sam, rest in my brother's room if you'd like. My parents won't know you're here if you're quiet. I have to deliver these loaves to the grog shop. And thanks for taking care of Gilgamesh." Enlil moved toward the door. "I'll return after my errands. We can talk more then."

After Enlil left, Sam brushed the remaining breadcrumbs closer to Gilgamesh. He hid his dagger beneath a corner of a sleeping mat and stretched out. He tried to sleep but couldn't. How could he, after what happened last night? Like letters carved onto a clay tablet, every moment seemed permanently etched in his memory. He let the events play out in his mind.

A rustling came from the bushes. Not seeing anything, he threw a rock, hoping to scare away whatever was there. As he prepared to throw a second rock, a snarl emerged from the bush. He froze. A small cheetah leapt out and pounced on his favorite lamb. Without thinking, he beat the cheetah with his staff. The cheetah turned to face him. It snarled once more, bared its teeth, and attacked him.

"Sam!" someone shouted.

Yasmah had returned!

His older brother dove into the cheetah with a dagger, saving him from the animal's claws. The cat, now wounded, turned on Yasmah. In the flickering firelight, he only saw the back of the cheetah's head and Yasmah's occasional lunges with the knife. Locked in a macabre dance, the two tumbled for a few moments. Then it ended. The cheetah lay dead, blood trickling from its neck.

He hurried over to where Yasmah lay. Blood oozed from his brother's side. His tattered tunic revealed where the cheetah had ripped into his chest and arms. Yasmah's breathing came hard and fast.

Sam whipped off his own cloak, pressed it against the wounds, and locked his gaze onto Yasmah's.

"Sam." Yasmah gasped for air. "I don't think I have much time. Listen carefully."

"Don't talk like that." Sam's voice cracked. "I'm good at fixing wounds." Tears mixed with dirt flowed down his checks. He didn't bother to wipe them.

Yasmah gripped his arm. "Listen, little brother. I went to Abzu' house to steal back our daggers. The ones Uncle Zim gave us before he left. I could only find one." Yasmah grit his teeth. He lifted the red-stained dagger he still clutched in his hand. "Take this and find Uncle Zim. He's all you have now. May the dagger bring you good luck."

"No! Don't say that." Sam grabbed Yasmah by the chin as he leaned over him. "We'll go to Uncle Zim together. You'll be fine. I'll take care of you."

Pain flooded Yasmah's eyes. He shook his head. "Reach inside my tunic."

Sam reached inside his brother's cloak and pulled out a small leather bag.

"It has jewels inside." Yasmah grit his teeth again. "I couldn't find our other dagger, but this bag was nearby so I took it. The jewels will buy you food and passage to Tyre. Fate has decreed it. Go now. Leave me." Yasmah squeezed his eyes shut.

"No, brother!" Sam shook Yasmah, hoping he'd open his eyes once more.

He didn't. Yasmah never moved or spoke again.

†††

Sam moaned and turned over on the sleeping mat. He imaged himself floating on a raft down the Tigris River. A cool breeze caressed his cheek as he watched the sun's reflection shimmer off the water. Without warning, clouds formed overhead. The sky darkened and lightning flashed. Rain pelted his raft. He struggled to stay afloat. A large wave washed over him, tossing him into the river's icy waters. As he went down for the third time, a paralyzing fear gripped him. No one would save him. He would die alone.

By the time Sam awoke, the Mesopotamian sun had risen to the middle of the early autumn sky. The warm rays brightened the room as they filtered in through the linen cloth covering the window. Trembling, Sam tried to shake off the dream. He rose to check Gilgamesh. The bird now hopped around the tabletop, pecking at the breadcrumbs.

Enlil emerged from behind a curtain on the other side of the room. He balanced a cup of tea in each hand. "I thought I would let you sleep." He placed the cups on the low table and sat on a mat. "You looked as if you needed to rest, but, now that you're awake, you can join me in a cup of barley tea."

Sam sat on a mat across from his new friend and gratefully sipped the warm brew.

"So, where in Susa does your uncle live?" Enlil asked.

"I-I am not sure." Sam wrapped his hands around his cup. He didn't know how much he wanted to reveal. Enlil was kind, but could he trust him?

Enlil cocked his head to one side. "What does your uncle do for a living?"

"He's a bronzeworker." Sam hesitated. "Actually, he doesn't exactly live here in Susa."

Enlil's dark eyebrows pinched together. "And your parents? You said they're both dead?"

"Ah, the truth is, my uncle actually lives in Tyre." Sam needed to avoid any discussion about his parents.

"I'm confused." Enlil shook his head. "I thought you said you came to the city to find your uncle after a cheetah attacked your sheep last night. If your parents are dead, and your uncle lives in Tyre, whose sheep were you watching?"

Sam also needed to avoid any discussion about the sheep's owner, their wicked landlord. "I didn't really say my uncle lives in Susa. What I meant was, I walked all night from the foothills of the Zagros Mountains so that I could *start* my search for my uncle here in Susa." Sam slurped his tea. "I hoped to find a caravan in Susa that I could take to Tyre."

Enlil's eyes narrowed. "It seems you don't even have money for food. How do you plan to pay for passage to Tyre? It's more than a month's journey west."

Clasping his cup between his hands, Sam swirled the remaining tea. "Can I trust you, Enlil?"

Enlil straightened and leaned closer. "Yes."

"To tell you the truth, the sheep I was watching belonged to our landlord. My father pledged my brother and me to him for a year of service to pay off our family's debts. My mother died while we were away. The landlord didn't even let us go home for her funeral. My older brother died last night trying to save me from the cheetah, so I ran away." Sam gulped the rest of his tea.

Enlil stared at Sam and didn't say a word.

Sam inhaled and continued. "Before my brother died, he gave me these." He reached inside his tunic and pulled out the pouch that hung from his neck. He emptied its contents onto the table. The facets of an emerald, diamond, and ruby glistened in the sun.

Enlil let out a low whistle. "I should say, any *one* of those jewels could pay your way to Tyre and back again. Several times."

"Do you know of any caravans leaving for Tyre?" Sam put the jewels back into his pouch.

"The gods must be with you." Enlil widened his eyes. "When I delivered bread to the grog shop this morning I heard that Negrel, a caravan driver, leaves tomorrow for Phoenicia. He spends every evening in the pub. You could meet him tonight and make your arrangements."

Sam nodded. "Yes, perhaps the gods *are* with me." He fingered the bronze dagger hidden under his cloak and recalled Yasmah's words. "May it bring you good luck."

CHAPTER 2

SAM MEETS AMATA

$\mathcal{E}$nlil stood. "I have several more deliveries this afternoon. You can stay here in my brother's room while I make them, but be very quiet. I'll be back before sundown and bring you supper. Then you can go and speak with the caravan driver. Like I said, my parents never come in here because they think it will bring bad luck, so no one will bother you."

Sam nodded. He had nowhere else to go, and the caravan wouldn't depart until tomorrow.

Enlil left to make his deliveries. After a short time, Sam grew restless. He fed Gilgamesh some bugs and placed a small dish of water next to the bird. With his dagger and jewels securely tucked within the folds of his tunic, he snuck out onto the streets of Susa.

Rays of the late afternoon sun fingered their way through the narrow streets and cast long shadows behind women hurrying home with market produce. A silversmith's stall caught Sam's attention. He stopped to admire the craftsman's work. He had once hoped to apprentice with his uncle as a bronzeworker, but that dream died when his uncle moved to Tyre. Still, he admired fine metalwork.

Sam picked up a small silver statue of the Babylonian god Shamash and examined it closely.

A few steps away stood a heavy-set man dressed in a white linen tunic. He had a red silk sash fastened around his waist. Sam gaped. He'd never seen such a well-dressed man.

The man in the white tunic gave the silversmith a handful of coins. "By the gods, Iggi," the rich looking man said. "You must be the finest silversmith in all of Mesopotamia."

"Many thanks, Zama." The silversmith smiled and bowed as he received his payment. "What is going on in Babylon these days? We don't get much news here in Susa."

"Ahh, have you not heard?" Zama raised his eyebrows. "The Great Hammurabi has erected a black, five-cubit high stone pillar displaying all his laws."

"Why would he do such a thing?"

"He has done this to force all the judges in Babylonia to apply the king's laws and decrees equally to all."

The silversmith gasped. "Never has such a thing been done."

"So true, Iggi." Zama nodded. "Hammurabi believes in justice. He also does not want any of his subjects to be ignorant of his laws. Now, if only all of his subjects could read!" Zama laughed, resting a hand his rotund stomach.

Iggi leaned closer to Zama. "So, what are some of the king's new laws?"

Sam moved behind a large clay statue and continued to listen.

"Let me see." Zama twirled the bottom hairs of his long gray beard. "The king has laws about women, slaves, the rich and the poor—they cover just about everyone."

Zama picked up a silver statue of the god, Marduk and studied it, holding it in midair. "You ask what some of the new laws are?" He continued to hold the statue aloft. "Let us say one of your customers took this silver statue without paying for it. One of Hammurabi's laws states that you could have the thief's hand cut off for stealing it. You could even demand his death for such a crime."

Sam gulped. Staring at the silver statue in his hand, he quickly returned it to the display table. He then touched his chest where the stolen jewels lay tucked inside his tunic. His stomach twisted.

Zama continued. "However, the new laws also state that you cannot be convicted of theft unless the stolen property is found in your possession." Zama smiled. "Yes, I dare say, our Great King Hammurabi wants to dispense justice equally to all." Zama bowed his head. "May Shamash lengthen his reign, and may King Hammurabi reign in righteousness over his subjects!"

Sam left the stall before the two men could notice him. He continued to explore the streets of Susa. The smell of cooked onions, fish, and barley cakes floated out of nearby homes and into the streets. The aromas brought back memories of meals he'd eaten at home. Memories that already seemed distant.

Sam neared a corner and was about to turn when he overheard several men's voices. He stopped in his tracks.

"I treated them like sons," a scratchy voice cried out. "And that was how they repaid me, by stealing my jewels and running away! The older one got himself killed by a cheetah. You can be sure their father will pay, every last shekel, he will."

"But, remember, Zaidu," a thin voice said. "Those jewels weren't yours to begin with!"

"Still, if I ever get my hands on the little urchin who stole them—"

Sam didn't wait to hear more. He turned and hobbled back to the bakery shop. In his hurry, he ran into a young girl exiting the loomery. The two collided, knocking both of them to the ground.

"I'm so sorry. I didn't see you." Sam struggled to stand. Once on his feet, he offered his hand to the girl who still lay sprawled out on the ground. "Are you all right?"

The girl sat but didn't look up. She cradled her elbow in her hand, winced, and finally eyed Sam. "I'm afraid I scraped my arm rather badly." A few drops of blood trickled out between her fingers.

"It's all my fault. I'm so sorry. Let me help you up." Sam helped her stand. Her braided hair, neatly pinned to her head, now threatened to break free from its restraints. He brushed a few pebbles from her yellow gown and pointed at her bleeding elbow. "I have an ointment that might help that feel better."

She arched an eyebrow. "Are you a healer?"

"No. I'm a shepherd. But if you come with me to the bakery shop, I think I can help."

"So you're a shepherd *and* a baker who also heals wounds?" The corners of her mouth curved up.

"Ah, no, I …"

She giggled. "It's all right. My father is a healer. He will take care of me when I get home."

Sam pointed to the bakery shop. "But we're so close. And I feel badly that I've injured you."

"Well, I suppose it will be okay. If it will make *you* feel better. But I'll have you know, I'm not in the habit of following strangers home." She smiled again.

Her sweet grin warmed his insides. "Oh, it's not my house. I'm just staying there with a friend."

When they reached the bakery, he led her in through the side door. He dampened a clean cloth and washed her wound. He picked up the gall nut from the table where he'd left it and applied the green sap to her cut. At first she pulled away, but then she let Sam spread it over the entire scrape.

"It feels cool," she said. "My name is Amata-Sukkal. Most people call me Amata. I don't think I've seen you before. What's your name?"

"Samsuluna. I'm only in Susa for a few days." He handed her the nut. "Here. Take this with you. Put some of its sap on your cut every day for the next week."

"Thank you. I hope to see you again before you leave." She lowered her head and slipped out the side door.

Sam sat to catch his breath. Was it meeting Amata that made his chest tight, or was it because he'd almost come face-to-face with his former landlord, Tu? Maybe both. Once again he slipped his dagger beneath a corner of the sleeping mat and tried to rest.

At sunset, Enlil brought Sam a barley cake and a small piece of cooked fish. Sam told Enlil about meeting Amata. He did not, however, tell him about Tu.

"Amata is the daughter of Balashi, one of Susa's finest asus," Enlil said. "She's rather pretty, isn't she?"

Sam face grew hot. "I-I hadn't noticed. I was too busy treating her cut." He took another bite of his barley cake and talked around the morsel. "What's an asu, anyway?"

"An asu is a healer." Enlil wiped his mouth with the back of his hand. "Balashi has become pretty famous in the last few months. Ever since he brought the governor's son back from a deadly illness."

After pulling a fishbone out of his mouth, Sam swallowed his last bite of fish. "So, tell me Enlil. How can I meet the caravan driver tonight? Did you leave word for him that I'm coming?"

Enlil nodded. "Yes. The grog shop owner said he'd tell Negrel to expect you. But let Negrel have a few drinks before you approach him. That'll put him in a better mood. And try to talk to him when he's alone. The men he hangs out with are nothing but trouble."

Sam grimaced. His father drank too, but waiting until he had several drinks never made his father more approachable. Just the opposite. Sam balled his fists and dug his fingernails dug into the palms of his hands. Drunk or sober, he'd approach Negrel tonight. The caravan was his only chance to find his uncle.

CHAPTER 3

THE CARAVAN DRIVER

*L*ater that evening, Sam made his way to the grog shop. When he asked about the caravan driver, the pub owner pointed out a burly man sitting at a table in the back. Negrel looked as if he hadn't bathed in months. Four husky men sat next to him—four ruffians who looked like men no one would dare to cross. Sam tightened the hemp rope belted around his waist and fingered the pouch of jewels hidden beneath his tunic. For good luck, he patted his hip where he always carried his bronze dagger.

The dagger!

In his rush to get to the grog shop he'd left it under the sleeping mat! His dinner rose to his throat. Should he get it before talking with Negrel? No. What if the man left before he got back? He lowered his head and approached the driver's table.

"I hear you're Negrel, the caravan driver," Sam's voice sounded louder than he'd intended.

Negrel turned and studied Sam. "What's it to ya?" The man gulped his grog, then wiped his sleeve across his greasy mustache and scraggly beard.

Sam stiffened his back, hoping to appear taller. "They say your caravan leaves tomorrow for Phoenicia. I want to go with you as far as Tyre." Something about the driver bothered Sam.

Negrel's left eye never looked straight at him. Instead, it looked off to the side.

The burly man belched in Sam's face. "I don't take children. I only take businessmen and merchandise." He waved a dismissive hand. "Go away. You annoy me."

Sam didn't budge. "Perhaps this will change your mind." He withdrew the ruby from his pouch.

The men around the table turned to eye Sam and his jewel. Negrel slowly reached for the ruby. Sam pulled it away. "You'll take me then?"

Negrel grabbed Sam's hand and wrenched the ruby from it. "Let me take a good look at that, boy." Negrel let out a slow whistle as he examined the gem. "Got any more like this?"

"That one jewel should be enough to buy me passage from here to Tyre and back again." Sam hoped he sounded assertive, but feared that his quivering voice betrayed his growing uneasiness.

The wooden bench scraped across the hardened dirt floor as Negrel stood. "Now, now, lad, nothin' to get upset about. I was just askin'." He grasped Sam's shoulder. "I prefer to make my business transactions outside. What say we step out into the night air and discuss my fees?"

Sam didn't have a chance to agree or refuse. Negrel's grip tightened as he pushed him out the door. The man glanced back and motioned his head as if telling his men to follow. He walked Sam out to the back of the grog shop. A few seconds later, Negrel's four friends joined them.

"You see, lad"—Negrel's face was so close to his, he nearly gagged on the man's ale-stenched breath—"my caravan's the only one headed for Tyre this month. That's why my fees is so high. If you want to deal with me, it'll cost ya more'n a jewel. What else have ya got?"

Sam studied the four bearded men that now closed in on

him. He squeezed his fingers around his walking stick. His tongue felt like sandpaper. With a shaking hand he pulled the emerald from his pouch and held it out. "This, this is all I've got. You can have it too if you promise to take me with you in your caravan tomorrow."

Negrel let out a wicked laugh. He snatched the emerald from Sam. "Well, boys, should I believe the little imp? Says this is all he's got!"

Sam bit the inside of his cheek and stepped back. *How could I have forgotten my dagger!*

A man with beady black eyes moved forward and grabbed Sam's arm. Sam slammed his walking stick into the man's shins and turned to run. Another man grabbed the back of his tunic. Sam jabbed the end of his stick into the second man's stomach. He ran around the side of the pub, hoping to make it to the door, but tripped over a rock. His stick flew out of his hand.

Someone grabbed his tunic again and yanked him to his feet. "I think we should teach this brat a lesson." Sam's captor dragged him back to Negrel.

The caravan driver locked his gaze onto Sam's. "First, boys, we search him. Says these two jewels is all he has. I don't believe him."

Sam twisted left then right as he tried to escape his captor's grasp, but it was no use. The beady-eyed man grabbed Sam's other arm. A third man untied the rope around Sam's waist as the fourth ruffian searched Sam and found the remaining jewel—a diamond.

"I'll show you what I do to them that lie to me." Negrel inhaled. His face turned red, as if it would explode. "They never lie to me again. Show him, lads." Negrel turned and walked away.

The four large men closed in. One slapped him in the face. Another landed a blow to his stomach. He lost count of the punches. The full moon dimmed. Everything went dark.

✝✝✝

The next thing Sam knew, water engulfed him. He felt as though his lungs would burst. He struggled to swim to the surface, but his arms wouldn't move. Was he submerged in a lake? A river? Somewhere in the distance, a familiar voice called out. His eyes flickered open, and he saw Enlil standing above him. Was it all a dream?

A light rain fell. When he tried to move, pain shot through his entire body, especially his right arm. As he came to his senses, he realized he lay in a puddle. Almost drowning had only been a dream. His beating, however, had been all too real. He must have been here all night.

"Sam!" Enlil bent down and shook his shoulder. "What happened to you?"

He tried to sit, but it only made the pain worse. As memories of last night's ordeal came to the forefront, his breath came in short gasps. "My jewels!" He moaned and slumped back into the puddle.

"You look terrible. Let me help you up." Enlil tried to lift Sam to his feet.

"Ahhh!" Pain shot through Sam's entire body. A damp cold penetrated him to the bone.

Enlil set Sam back on the ground. He then grabbed Sam's tunic at the shoulders and dragged him out of the puddle. Taking off his own cloak, Enlil placed it over Sam. "Try to stay warm, friend. I'll get Balashi and hurry back."

Sam pulled Enlil's cloak more closely around him and fell back asleep. He had no idea how much time elapsed before he felt strong arms lift him and carry him away.

The next time Sam opened his eyes he found himself in a

warm bed. When he tried to brush hair out of his face, he discovered his right arm in a splint. It was snugly wrapped in a white linen bandage. He attempted to take a deep breath but couldn't. Looking at his chest, he saw it was also wrapped in linen. "Wh-what happened? Where am I?"

Amata's gentle face, framed by her long black hair, appeared above him. "Here, sip this." She slowly raised his head and pressed a cup to his lips.

The warm liquid soothed his dry throat.

"You've slept for two days." Amata explained. "My father says you have a broken arm and broken ribs." She felt his forehead. "At least your fever's down."

Sam tried to sit, but the pain in his chest made him fall back onto the pillow. "My jewels." He groaned.

"That's all you've said for the past two days." Amata placed his cup on a night stand. "What are you talking about?"

Sam tried to pull in a breath, but only a puff entered his lungs. His head felt light. With the jewels gone, he had no way to reach Uncle Zim. *What am I going to do now?* Amata's face began to fade. He closed his eyes and fell back asleep.

† † †

The next day when Sam awoke, Enlil sat on a chair next to his bed. "I brought your bronze dagger." Enlil handed it to him. "You left it under the sleeping mat."

Sam frowned. "I know." He slipped the cold metal beneath his pillow. "If I had remembered to take it with me the night I met Negrel, maybe I would have had better luck fighting off his men." Sam's gaze met Enlil's. "You haven't said anything to Amata or her father about Negrel, have you?"

Enlil pressed his lips together and shook his head no. "I haven't told them much of anything about you. I figured you'd tell them when you were ready."

"Thanks." Sam nodded. "You've been a true friend, Enlil. Living in the Zagros Mountains, I didn't have any friends except my brother. And now he's gone."

"And so are your jewels. You kept muttering about them when you had your fever. What'll you do now?"

Sam's blinked several times. "I-I really don't know. There's nothing for me back home, and I've no way to get to Tyre."

"Would you two care for some tea?" Amata entered the room carrying a tray. "Father says you should only stay a few more minutes, Enlil. Sam needs more rest."

"Actually, I should be going now." Enlil stood to leave. "I'm already late for my deliveries. I'll check in with you again tomorrow, Sam. I'm glad you're feeling better."

Enlil bowed to Amata. "May the gods look kindly on your household. Many thanks to you and your father for helping Sam."

✝✝✝

Three weeks later, Sam sat on a cushion at a low, beautifully carved cedar table across from Balashi and Amata. A servant in a white linen robe placed bowls of chicken soup in front of them. Sam stared across the table at the stern-looking face of his host. Studying the healer's dark brown beard peppered with strands of gray, he wondered if a soft face hid behind it.

"I'm grateful for your hospitality." Sam fingers trembled as he lifted silver spoon. "I don't know how I can ever repay you."

"And I am grateful for the gall nut you gave my daughter." Balashi sipped his soup and said no more.

Except for the slurping of soup, all remained silent for several minutes. Finally, Amata spoke. "Sam, my arm is almost completely healed. Father says he's never seen a wound heal so quickly. He's tried the gall nut on several of his patients and experienced the same quick-healing results."

Balashi cleared his throat and glanced at Amata. She didn't speak again.

Sam glanced from Amata to Balashi. Both stared into their bowls of chicken soup as they slowly finished their meal. Perhaps it was their custom to eat in silence. Sam did the same.

The following week, Balashi removed the bandages from Sam's chest and invited him out into the garden for a walk.

"So, you tell me you are an orphan who left his shepherding occupation to come and find your uncle here in Susa." Sam followed Balashi down a dirt path between a row of leafless autumn trees. "Now that you are almost healed, how do you plan to find him? Do you know where he lives?"

Sam swallowed. "Well, sir, he, he doesn't really live here in Susa. He actually lives in Tyre."

"Hmm, I see." After stopping to examine his thyme and sage plants, the asu continued his stroll. "And how do you plan to get to Tyre? And how did you come to have a broken arm and ribs? You have never really explained this to me since we found you outside the grog shop."

Heat flamed Sam's face. He hadn't told Amata or her father anything about the stolen jewels or his dagger, and he'd sworn Enlil to secrecy. How much could he trust his new friends? Balashi had been so kind to take care of him, and, until now, had asked few questions. He scrambled to think of an answer.

"I'm not really sure how my accident happened, sir." Sam's insides twisted as the lie tumbled out of his mouth. "I had a fever when I reached the city of Susa and went to the grog shop hoping to find food. The next thing I knew, you found me and nourished me back to health. I am eternally grateful. As I've said, I don't know how I can ever repay you."

"Well, you seem to have an interest, perhaps even a natural talent in the healing arts," Balashi said. "Perhaps you would consider becoming my apprentice? I could use some help in my work."

Balashi continued to walk down the path, hands clasped behind his back, but Sam froze in his tracks.

"You would consider making me your apprentice?"

Balashi stopped and turned to glance back at Sam. For the first time, Sam saw a gentle kindness behind the asu's dark brown eyes. "You have told me that you are an orphan and have no way to make the long journey to Tyre where your uncle lives." Balashi raised his hands and shrugged his shoulders. "As I said, I have been very busy, especially since I healed the governor's son. I, like you, search for natural ways to cure my patients. Since more of my patients seem to recover than those of other asus, more and more people seek my help. So, perhaps will you consider my offer?"

Sam couldn't believe his ears. For the past week he'd felt as though a dark cloud hovered over him. He'd moped around the doctor's house, wondering what he'd do after he recovered. Without the jewels, he had no way to get to Tyre. He couldn't go back to shepherding, and he certainly wouldn't go back to his drunken father. And now, the doctor had offered to make him an apprentice!

CHAPTER 4

The River

Days turned into months. One cool spring morning, Sam joined Amata in collecting balls of sap from the Nummlaria plants in Balashi's garden. Just as Balashi had taught him, Sam slipped the congealed, pea-sized balls into sacks of barley flour for safekeeping,

"Amata, come over here," Sam called out. "Look at this strange thing I just found in my barley sack!" He motioned her over to his side of the garden.

Amata hiked up her gown above her ankles and rushed over. "What is it?" She gazed at his flour-filled hand and frowned. "I don't see anything."

"Here." Sam raised his palm closer to her face and pointed to several balls of sap half-buried in the flour. "Look closer."

Amata bent over until her nose almost touched his palm.

Sam inhaled, as if to sneeze. "Ah, ah." Rubbing his nose, he forced out a blast of air. "Aw-choo!"

Flour-dust sprayed everywhere, especially onto Amata's face.

Pointing at her, he bent back, laughing. "You look like a ghost traveling to the netherworld!"

"Very funny, Samsuluna!" She landed a light, playful kick to his shin. "If you would stop fooling around and help me finish this, maybe Father will let us join Enlil down at the river before it gets too late. Remember? Enlil said he finished making his raft. He told us to join him for a trip downriver if we finished our work early today."

Sam had almost forgotten. So much had changed over the past few months. For the first time in his life, he had friends. In the mornings, Amata usually worked at her loom while he met with a tutor who taught him how to read. In the afternoons, Sam accompanied Balashi to visit patients. In the early evenings before dinner, he, Amata, and Enlil often played board games together or raced down to the river. Sam couldn't remember when he'd felt happier. The dark cloud that had always loomed overhead seemed to have vanished.

"Samsuluna!" Balashi shouted from the house. "I need those Nummlaria balls. Immediately. We must visit the Priest of Nintu. His servant came by to say the priest is complaining again of severe stomach cramps."

Retrieving his barley sack from the ground, Sam tied the top into a knot. He then glanced at Amata's powder-gray face. He swallowed a chuckle but couldn't resist flashing her a lopsided grin. "Hopefully, I can meet you and Enlil by the river if this visit doesn't take too long."

†††

Their visit with the priest lasted longer than Sam expected. The Priest of Nintu insisted that Balashi treat his wife and daughter who also complained of stomach cramps. After giving everyone the Nummlaria medicine, the priest asked Sam and Balashi to join him at the ziggurat for a thanksgiving offering to the mother goddess, Nintu. To refuse would offend the priest and his family, so Balashi agreed. By the time they left the ziggurat it was well past midday.

Walking home beside Balashi, Sam noted the elongated

shadows trailing the merchants that passed by. He shifted the asu's medicine pouch to his other shoulder. *Amata and Enlil spent the afternoon on the raft without me.* He kicked a rock. This past week, he'd rarely had any free time to join his friends.

"So, my young apprentice," Balashi interrupted Sam's thoughts. "If we use the Nummlaria sap to heal stomach cramps, do you recall what we use for coughs and chest pains?"

Mashing his lips together, Sam thought for a moment. "I remember that when we visited Judge Mera last week, you gave him droppings from the Teasel plant. I saw the judge yesterday, and he said his coughing has stopped, and he feels much better."

Balashi smiled. "You learn quickly, Samsuluna."

Although he appreciated Balashi's praise and was grateful to work as his apprentice, he still wished he had more free time. He kicked another rock that begged to be moved further down the road. "Sir," Sam asked, "why don't you believe in seeking the gods' help with your healings, like other asus?"

Balashi's colorful robe flowed around him, twirling up curls of dust, but the man remained silent as they continued to walk.

Nearby, a crow cawed.

Sam paused and glanced up. He spotted the large bird at the top of a nearby palm.

Joining Sam in his study of the crow, Balashi also gazed up.

The crow swiveled its head down, as if searching for a meal. Apparently not seeing any, it flapped its large black wings and flew to another palm.

The scene reminded Sam of a story his tutor had told him earlier that week. Since Balashi hadn't answered his previous question as to why he didn't seek the gods' help in healing his patients, he took another tack. "Sir, do you believe in the stories about the ancient gods?"

Once again, no answer came from the asu. He only stood staring up at the crow.

With the taste of dry dust in his mouth, Sam's curiosity also dried up. *How can I learn anything from Amata's father if he never answers my questions?*

Finally, Balashi spoke. "Samsuluna, do you have a particular story about the gods in mind?"

Sam scratched his head and pressed forward. "Yes, sir, I do. Earlier this week, my tutor told me about the legendary Sumerian hero, Gilgamesh. He said Gilgamesh had an ancient relative named Ut-na-pish-tim. I found this story hard to believe, but, supposedly, the gods once told Ut-na-pish-tim to build a large boat to save his family and relatives from a worldwide flood that the gods were about to send upon the earth."

Sam glanced at the nearby palm where the crow had landed, then continued. "After the storm, Ut-na-pish-tim's boat rested on a mountain. My tutor said he sent out a dove to see if the floodwaters had gone down. But when the dove didn't find any food, it returned to the boat.

"My tutor also said the same thing happened when Ut-na-pish-tim sent out a swallow. It also returned because it couldn't find any food. The floodwaters were still too high. After waiting several more weeks, he finally sent out a crow. When the crow didn't return, Ut-na-pish-tim knew he and the others could safely leave the boat." Sam glanced at the crow once more. "If that story is true, then maybe seeing this crow today will bring me good luck."

Balashi watched as the crow cawed, then flew off into the distance. He motioned for Sam to continue walking. "Our people believe in luck and in the fate the gods deal out to us," Balashi said. "I suppose, however, that I take after one of my ancient relatives, Abram."

Balashi continued to talk as they passed a man digging in his front garden. "Abram could not go along with the idea of thousands of gods, such as a god who watches over your shovel, a goddess who watches over your cooking, a god of the water, one for the sky, the moon, war, the underworld, and so on. He believed in only one God. It has been said that Abram believed his God told him to take his family and move west to Canaan. Abram didn't believe in luck or fate. He believed in obeying his God, and that his God was his friend. His faith in only one God intrigues me. Perhaps I will go to Canaan someday and find out more for myself."

Sam's pulse quickened at the thought of his mentor throwing aside the traditions of the Babylonian people. "So, you believe in this one God of Abram?"

"Right now, I don't believe in any gods." Balashi shrugged. "Mind you, I keep this to myself. I go along with our rituals to stay in favor with the rulers and my patients. Unlike most asus, however, I don't think luck, fate, or unseen gods have anything to do with healing. I suppose that is why I seek natural cures for my patients." Balashi patted the leather pouch slung over Sam's shoulder. "That is why we carry many more medicines with us than any of the other asus."

Sam turned Balashi's words over in his mind as they finished their journey home. He didn't agree with Balashi about there being no such thing as luck or fate. Certainly, he'd been born into an unlucky family. But now, as Yasmah had said the night he died, the bronze dagger had brought him good luck. Becoming Balashi's apprentice, having a roof over his head, and being able to call Amata and Enlil his friends, surely these evidenced the good fate brought on by his lucky dagger, and perhaps the gods, or the one God of Abram. And now, the appearance of the crow would bring him more good luck.

By the time Sam reached the river, Enlil and Amata were nowhere in sight. The late afternoon sun danced brightly off the water, inviting Sam for a swim. He dove into the cool water and swam out to his favorite rock.

Stretching out in the sun, he recalled some of the conversations he'd had with Enlil and Amata over the past few months. Enlil had shared a secret desire to become a caravan driver and see the world. Enlil admitted, however, this was only a dream. One day, it would be his responsibility to take over his family's bakery business.

Amata shared special memories of her mother who had died when Amata was only six years old. She died from an illness even Balashi couldn't heal. After suffering with a high fever for two weeks, her mother passed away. "That's when father stopped believing in the gods." Amata sighed. Her face darkened, but then brightened slightly. "Just before she died," Amata continued, "my mother sang my favorite lullaby." Amata's lilting voice sang the tender words.

> *"Little one who once dwelt in darkness,*
> *you have now seen the light of day.*
> *Why the crying, why the worries?*
> *What has made your peace undone..."*

Sitting on the rock, Sam hummed the melody Amata taught them that day. Before he reached the end of the tune, the sound of laughter drifted over the water. Lifting his head, he saw Enlil and Amata returning on Enlil's bamboo raft.

Sam stood and shouted from his rock-island. "Hey! Over here!"

Enlil and Amata continued to talk and laugh without glancing in his direction.

As if clouds had suddenly covered the sun, a chill ran through him. He looked up. There were no clouds. *Why didn't they wait for me?* A rock formed in his stomach.

Slipping into the water, Sam swam out to the raft.

As Amata and Enlil chattered on, Sam reached their craft and pushed up on its side. Giving another hard shove, he flipped the raft over.

Plunging into the water, Amata screamed.

Enlil toppled in backwards and flayed his arms. "By the gods," he shouted. Enlil reached out and grabbed the edge of the raft.

Sam threw his head back and laughed as he treaded water. "You two didn't even see me coming, did you?" He grabbed Enlil's paddle before it drafted away, then helped Enlil and Amata onto the raft.

Once all three had settled aboard, Amata narrowed her eyes and gave Sam a look that seemed to shoot darts at him. "That was a mean thing to do, Samsuluna." She slowly glanced away and squeezed excess water from her long, black braid.

"Oh, come on." Sam waved a hand. "If you don't want to get wet, don't get in the water. I was just having a little fun."

Enlil paddled toward the shore. "Just having fun?" After a few more strokes, Enlil set down his bamboo oar, lunged toward Sam, and pushed him into the river. "There. Now, you can have even more fun!"

Taken by surprise, Sam thrashed around, gulped in a mouthful of water, and went under. Struggling back to the surface, he heard Amata and Enlil laughing. He reached out to scramble back onto the raft.

Instead of helping him, Enlil widened the distance between him and the raft as he swiftly paddled toward shore.

Sam swam in alone.

Once he reached the riverbank, Sam stayed near the shore while Enlil dragged the raft to a nearby cove and covered it with palm branches.

"I'd better get home now," Enlil told Amata. "Maybe I'll see you tomorrow."

Enlil didn't bother saying goodbye to Sam.

"What's *his* problem?" Sam kicked a rock as he and Amata walked home together.

"He didn't appreciate your little joke," Amata said without turning to look at Sam. "And neither did I."

Sam didn't see much of Amata or Enlil over the next few weeks. Balashi kept him busy visiting patients. Sam assisted the asu in sewing stitches, bandaging wounds, and mixing and administering medicines.

One day, after treating a wound the governor had sustained while hunting, Sam accompanied Balashi to the apothecary shop. The asu picked out several new herbs he wanted to try. After placing them on the low counter, he removed a leather cord from around his neck. A small cylindrical clay seal with the imprint of a bull dangled from the cord. Balashi handed the seal to the short, bald shopkeeper. "Avara, please use my seal to show that I owe you for these herbs. I would like to take them now and settle my account with you at the end of the month."

"Very good, Balashi," the shopkeeper said. After bowing low, Avara rolled Balashi's seal onto a moist clay table. "Your seal is always welcome here."

Balashi turned to Sam. "I am going to give you a copy of my seal to wear around your neck as well, Samsuluna. Then, if I ever send you on an errand to purchase goods for me, you may use my seal to pay for them." Balashi withdrew a duplicate leather cord and seal from within his tunic and fastened it around Sam's neck.

Sam's chest tightened. "I am not worthy of such a privilege, sir." Thinking of the lies he'd told the good asu, Sam grasped the cord and lifted it from around his neck. "I'm just a crippled orphan. I've done nothing to deserve such trust."

Grasping Sam's hands, Balashi shook his head. "Trust is earned, Samsuluna, and you have earned my trust."

Blood pounded in Sam's ears, drowning out all other sounds. He wanted to run out of the shop. Run down the street. Run out of the city and back to the mountains. But then again, he couldn't run any longer. The best he could do was a fast limp. Maybe he should just confess all his lies right here and now.

Too ashamed, he decided against that too. Instead, he gazed down at his dusty sandals and said nothing. He left the seal around his neck and shuffled out of the shop behind Balashi, doubting he'd ever live up to the man's trust.

After their evening meal, Sam retired with Balashi to the sitting room where they reviewed clay tablets that a servant had recently brought back from Egypt. The tablets spoke of new herbs and claimed that they reduced fevers.

"Look here, Samsuluna." Balashi pointed to markings on one of the tablets. "This describes a fever similar to the one Amata's mother had before she died." The older man's voice quickened. "It says here that the herb—"

"Father?"

Balashi cut his sentence short as Amata entered.

Sam shifted his gaze from Balashi's tablet to a wooden board Amata held in her hands.

"Father," she repeated, "would you play the Royal Game of Ur with me?" She offered a sly grin. "I might even let you win this time."

Sam stood to get a closer look at the gameboard. In the Zagros Mountains, his family never had time for leisure activities. The three-squared board, decorated with a rosette, intrigued him. Maybe Amata would teach him how to play. Sam glanced over at Balashi.

Without gazing up from his clay tablet, Amata's father waved a dismissive hand. "Not now, dear. Sam and I are reviewing some new remedies. Perhaps tomorrow evening."

"Yes Father." Amata lowered her eyes. "I understand."

Sam's shoulders tensed. What did she mean, she *understood*?

He certainly found it hard to understand *her*. Growing up with a brother and no sisters, girls confused him.

Before she turned to leave, her gaze met his. Her eyes narrowed. Once again, those dark orbs shot out darts. Darts meant for him, that hit their mark.

She stiffly turned and strode away.

CHAPTER 5

THE MARKETPLACE

Late the next afternoon, in the stifling heat, Sam shuffled to the market. Even though they had just finished a long, exhausting day visiting the sick, Balashi sent him out to buy more fish for dinner. It seemed they were to have an unexpected guest, and their cook Eshe was too busy preparing for his arrival to make the additional purchase.

Sam limped his way through the alleys and streets of Susa, struggling to breathe. As he passed the mud-brick homes where some of the wealthier residents lived, he smelled lamb roasting somewhere over a fire. When given a choice, he'd much rather have lamb than fish. But, thank the gods, he couldn't complain. At least he had food every day and a roof over his head.

The winding streets took Sam through a neighborhood where the homes stood closely packed together. A new scent filled the air. It made his mouth water. The image of his mother suddenly formed in his mind. His mother stirring a pot of turtle soup. Someone here was making it with the same herbs and spices his mother had used. Those days seemed long ago.

As Sam neared the marketplace, he reviewed the past few weeks. He and Balashi had never been so busy. Was that why he and Amata hadn't talked much lately? Or was there something else? Ever since he had dumped her into the water, she'd grown distant. Girls. How was he supposed to understand them? If he and Yasmah had a problem, they worked it out by punching or wrestling with each other. He figured that wouldn't work with Amata.

Before long, Sam found himself at the bazaar in front of the fish market stall. He picked out a few carp and catfish, then handed Balashi's seal to the fishmonger.

The seller pressed the seal into wet clay, wrapped the fish in date palm leaves, and handed him the package.

Suddenly, off to his left, Sam spied Amata at a jewelry stall. She was examining a lapis lazuli necklace.

The necklace entranced him. Strung between the highly polished blue stones lay pebbles of gold pyrite that sparkled in the sunlight.

Amata sighed and handed the necklace back to the merchant. As she turned to leave, her gaze met Sam's.

He strode over. "Are you going back home now, Amata?"

"I have one more stop." She glanced at the necklace again. "I have to retrieve a tunic and a shawl from the loomery."

"If you'd like, I could go with you and help you carry the packages," Sam said. "Balashi sent me out to buy more fish for tonight's dinner." He held up the date palm leaves that encased the fish.

Amata shrugged. "If you wish." She turned and traipsed toward the loomery.

He followed along in silence.

When they arrived at the loomery, an elderly seamstress held up a white linen dress for Amata's inspection.

"It's beautiful." Amata slowly nodded and smiled.

"Let's make sure it's the right length." The seamstress held the garment up against Amata. "Yes, that looks perfect, dear. When wearing this," she said, still holding the dress up to Amata, "you gather it on your left shoulder where you can clip it or make a tie loop to hold it in place. And, as I'm sure you know, you wear it off your shoulder on the right. Fasten your favorite belt around your waist, add a few pieces of select jewelry, and you'll turn many heads!"

Amata blushed.

Pretending not to notice, Sam turned his attention to other garments suspended from a pole across the back of the shop. He admired the quality of the flaxen linens, remembering the coarse flaxen garments he'd worn when he lived in the Zagros Mountains.

"What about the shawl?" Amata asked as she took the gown from the seamstress and laid it on a wooden table next to her.

"I think you will be pleased." The seamstress smiled. She went behind a curtain and then returned with a blue linen shawl. She placed it around Amata's shoulders. The edges flowed down below her waist.

Amata fingered the golden fringe encompassing the shawl's hemline. "It's beautiful." She pulled the cloak more firmly around her shoulders and lightly brushed her hand over the softened linen.

Sam gazed at Amata. "Yes, it is." He wasn't referring only to the shawl.

Once again, Amata's cheeks brightened. She glanced at Sam. A faint smile crossed her face, then quickly faded.

"Now, what about slippers?" the seamstress interrupted. "I have gold ones here that match your shawl's fringe." She pointed to a delicate set of footwear on another table. "Or, perhaps you would prefer these blue ones?" She held up a blue-dyed pair of woolen slippers with leather bottoms. "They are both your size."

Amata tried on the blue woolen slippers. "Yes, these will do." She removed Balashi's seal from around her neck and paid for the merchandise.

The seamstress wrapped the gown and shawl in a flaxen cloth and then did the same with the slippers.

"Here, I'll carry those for her," Sam offered.

Amata grasped Sam's arm. "I'll take the gown and shawl package," she said. "Why don't you just carry the shoes? I don't want the garments to pick up any fish odor."

As they left the shop, Sam asked, "What are these beautiful garments for? Do you have a special occasion coming up?"

"Father heard rumors that he might get a promotion," she said. "If he does, it'll be announced at a special ceremony, and we'll all be invited. He's fairly certain of the new position, so he suggested I buy myself a new gown for the event." Amata hesitated and then added, "Actually, I think he was just trying to cheer me up."

The two returned home in silence. Before they entered the house, they both spoke at once.

"Sam."

"Amata."

"You can go first." Sam laughed. "Even though you're a girl." He grinned.

Amata studied the ground and bit her lower lip. Finally, her gaze meet Sam's. "I'm sorry I haven't talked to you much lately. I've been feeling a little—oh—I don't exactly know what I've been feeling. I guess that's my problem." Amata grimaced and fell silent again.

"I'm sorry about the raft." Sam shook his head. "I didn't mean to hurt your feelings. I only meant it as a joke."

"I guess that's part of it." Amata shifted the package in her hands. "I was enjoying my time with Enlil, and then you inter-rupted us." Amata rolled in her lips before she continued. "You and Father spend a lot of time together. I feel left out. I was trying to explain that to Enlil when you flipped over the raft."

Sam scratched his head. "I don't understand."

"That's just it Sam." Amata shook her head. "You don't understand." She wrinkled her nose. "It seems like you walk around with a cloud over your head. I feel like you only share a small part of yourself with us, all the while holding back some dark secret. It seems you don't trust us, or anybody. You're like a bird with a broken wing. You traipse around the city with Father, healing the sick, but you can't seem to heal yourself."

Sam swallowed hard. No one had ever been so blunt with him. "And what does Enlil think?" His throat tightened. "Does he feel the same way?"

"Enlil believes you trust him more than anyone," she said, "but he thinks you don't fully trust him either. He wants to be your friend, but he doesn't know what else to do."

A burning rose in his chest. His nose tingled. "You're right. I don't trust people. I guess I don't know how."

He wondered if he ever would.

CHAPTER 6

THE MESSENGER

A messenger from Babylon arrived a few days later as Sam ate his afternoon meal with Amata and Balashi. One of Balashi's servant escorted him into the dining room. Bowing low, the courier handed Balashi a clay tablet. "I come directly from Hammurabi's court, sir."

Stroking his brown and gray peppered beard, Balashi read the tablet to himself.

Eternity seemed to pass. Sam wanted to blurt out, *What does it say?* but held his tongue.

Finally, Balashi lifted his gaze. "I have been offered a position as a court physician in Babylon." The corners of the elderly man's eyes crinkled. "I heard rumors I might receive such an invitation. News of my healing work here in Susa has spread to the court, and the king's physicians want me to come to Babylon as soon as possible."

Balashi turned to the messenger. "Tell the court physicians they can expect my reply by the end of the week."

The messenger bowed and left.

"May I read the message, Father?" Amata asked.

Balashi nodded and slid the tablet across the cedar tabletop.

Sam's chest swelled as he watched Amata read the message.

Well-to-do fathers trained their sons to read, not their daughters. Usually, daughters were only trained to cook, weave, garden, and care for children. Balashi, however, was not a usual father.

As Amata read the cuneiform figures carved into the clay tablet, Sam studied her expression. Nothing changed. He couldn't tell if she felt happy or sad about the news.

"You mentioned you might get a promotion." Amata pressed her lips into a flat line, then continued. "But I thought it would be a special position here in Susa, not the capital. Would you really consider moving to Babylon?" She handed the tablet back to her father.

Setting it next to him, he reached into the large fruit bowl in the middle of the table. He withdrew a fig and chewed slowly before he answered. "Amata, moving to Babylon could open many doors for us."

Frowning, Amata pressed her palms on the table and leaned forward. "What you really mean, Father, is that this could be a good opportunity for you and Sam." Her pitch raised. "But I have many friends here in Susa, and you have more than enough patients. Why do you need to go to Babylon? I don't want to leave our home. I don't want to move away from the memories I have here of Mother."

Balashi's forehead furrowed. "We must consider what's best for all of us." He studied his daughter's reddening face, then continued. "We will talk more of this later. Right now, I have something I need to discuss with both of you." Clearing his throat, he leaned toward Sam. "Son, you have done a wonderful job as my apprentice. How would you like to become part of our family?"

Taken by surprise, Sam widened his eyes. "You mean you want to adopt me?"

"That's right, my boy." Balashi crossed his arms leaned back. "Since your parents are dead, and you aren't really sure how to find your uncle, I would like to officially adopt you as my son."

Sam's head spun. Adopted by the great asu? A possible move to the capital city? Perhaps continue his apprenticeship with Balashi in the king's court? By the gods, how could he be so lucky?

But then, like demons from the netherworld, the half-truths he'd told Amata and Balashi rose to accuse him. He was not worthy of such luck. He was just a poor, orphaned cripple from the Zagros Mountains. His stomach churned and cramped. Undigested food from his afternoon meal rose to his throat, discharging a sour, bitter taste in his mouth. Searching Amata's face for a clue as to how she'd taken the news, he found none.

Suddenly, Amata burst into tears and ran from the room.

Sam stood, gripped his walking stick, and bowed to Balashi. "By the gods, sir, taking me on as your apprentice was more than I deserved. But, adopting me as your son?" Sam paused, fearing his heart would beat out of his chest. "No. I am not worthy to be your son." He lowered his gaze. "You and Amata deserve better. And, may the gods forbid, I would never want to come between you two."

Balashi stood and stepped near Sam. "I will speak with Amata. Perhaps, for her, this is too much too soon." He placed his hand on Sam's shoulder. "I have come to love you like a son, Samsuluna. I know you have the potential to become a great asu, and I want to help you develop your talents."

Clearing his throat, Balashi continued. "True love is something that is freely given, not earned. A father loves his children not because he deems them worthy, but because they are his children. That is why I want to adopt you. I want to bestow that kind of love on you, Sam, just as I have for Amata."

A mist clouded Balashi's eyes. "On the other hand," he continued, "trust is something that can be earned—or lost. You, Samsuluna, have earned my trust. And now, not because of that trust, but with the love of a father, I would like to adopt you as part of our family. Think on it, son. I will speak with Amata, and we will discuss it again at the end of the week."

Over the next few days, Amata seemed to purposely avoid Sam. Whenever he found an opportunity to talk with her, she'd shrug her shoulders and walk away. He reminded himself that, since the age of six, her family had only included two people—Amata and her father. How could he ask her to expand that bond to include him, a virtual stranger? And yet, Balashi had spoken of a fatherly love—a love freely given, not based on worth. Did such a thing really exist? Not in his experience.

After six days of tension between him and Amata, Sam couldn't sleep. Balashi would soon bring up the adoption question again. What should he say? He tossed and turned on his sleeping mat. Should he tell them the truth, that his father wasn't really dead? That he just wished he was? How he ached to be part of a family where he was wanted and appreciated, not berated and beaten.

However, it seemed Amata wasn't thrilled with the idea of him joining their family of two. If only he hadn't lost his jewels. If he still had them, he'd slip away into the night and resume his search for his uncle. No. He didn't have the money for that. At least, not yet. Last month, Balashi began paying him an allowance for his work as an apprentice. He said the amount would increase as Sam's skills increased. It would probably take at least a year before he earned enough to join a caravan to Tyre. He needed an immediate answer to his problem.

Sam doubted they'd understand, but, by morning, he'd made up his mind. Without telling anyone, he would "borrow" money from Balashi in order to buy passage to Tyre. Once he found his uncle and started earning his own way, he'd repay the good doctor.

The next day, Sam waited until everyone fell asleep. When all was quiet, he crept to the cabinet where Balashi kept his coins. He counted out fifteen shekels and placed them in the leather pouch around his neck. With his heart in his throat, he patted the dagger beneath his tunic, took one last look around the house, and disappeared into the night.

CHAPTER 7

BABYLON

By the time the sun rose to mid-morning, Sam reached the town of Tepe Guran. When he passed a bakery, the yeasty smell of freshly-baked bread made his stomach growl. He reached for the pouch of coins around his neck, then stopped. Should he spend the money? He might need all of it for passage to Tyre.

He grasped the leather cord and was reminded that two cords encircled his neck. Yes! He still wore Balashi's seal. He and Balashi had visited Tepe Guran once before. The merchants here accepted the asu's seal as credit. He turned back to the bakery shop.

After waiting for the two soldiers in front of him to order their goods, he stepped up to the baker. "Two loaves of bread, please." He removed the leather cord with Balashi's seal and handed it to the owner.

The baker, a heavy-set man, wrinkled his nose and squinted his eyes as he studied the small cylindrical seal. "So, the Great Balashi wants this on his account, does he? Just a minute, lad. Let me finish up with my other customers."

Sam looked over the bakery goods on display as the owner handed the soldiers their order. A minute later, a dark shadow fell over Sam.

"Where did you get this seal, boy?" One of the soldiers thrust Balashi's seal in front of Sam's face.

"Please, sir." He turned to face the soldier. "I-I am an apprentice of the great asu, Balashi. He gave me his seal to make purchases for him."

"Well, I think you should come with us until we can verify your story with the asu." The soldier grabbed Sam's arm.

He had no choice but to go with him.

The soldiers searched Sam and confiscated his fifteen shekels and bronze dagger. He spent the rest of the day in a cold, damp cellar.

By evening, a guard came and ushered Sam upstairs to a waiting area. A few minutes later, another soldier entered, accompanied by Balashi. Filled with shame and embarrassment, Sam couldn't even raise his head to look at the man.

"Well, Samsuluna," Balashi said as he sat next to Sam on a stone bench. "I wondered why you hadn't returned home yet with the bread I sent you to fetch."

Sam shot Balashi a puzzled look.

The soldier that had brought Sam upstairs clapped Balashi's shoulder. "You'd have us believe you sent this boy all the way from Susa to Tepe Guran to buy a loaf of bread?"

"Ah." Balashi raised a finger. "But, it is very special bread." A playful grin stretched across Balashi's bearded face. "And besides that, I also gave young Samsuluna fifteen shekels to purchase special medicines that can only be found in Tepe Guran's apothecary shop." The asu glanced at Sam with twinkling eyes, then turned back to the soldiers. "Sirs, I think you have wasted enough of our time. Would you please release the boy now into my care?"

It was too late to walk back to Susa that evening, so Balashi rented a room at an inn for the night.

Sam finally broke the silence as they entered their sleeping quarters. "Why didn't you tell the soldiers the truth?" he asked.

"And what truth is that?" Balashi moved to the ceramic water basin near the bedside and washed his face.

"The truth that I ran off with your money and your seal. I slipped away to find a caravan going to Tyre so I could search for my uncle." Sam removed his dusty sandals and outer tunic.

Balashi dried his face and hands before he spoke. "Samsuluna, I care for you as if you were my own son. Everything I have is yours. If you do not want me to adopt you, if you would rather go to Tyre and find your uncle, just say so. I want what is best for you."

Sam's lower lip quivered. He'd never known such love and acceptance. Tears leaked from the corners of his eyes. "But I don't deserve your love and trust." His nose burned.

"Children don't have to deserve their parents' love." Still wearing his woolen-heeled sandals, Balashi padded over to Sam and brushed a few bangs out of his eyes. "As I mentioned before, parents love their children because they are their children. And as I also said before, trust can be earned—and lost. Taking off with my shekels and seal, I admit, has shaken my trust in you. If you choose to become part of our family, we will have to work on rebuilding that trust."

Sam couldn't hold back the flood. He let his tears fall. Wrapping his arms around Balashi, he buried his face in the gentle man's robe. "But Amata is your true child, not me." He sobbed. "She doesn't want you to adopt me. Don't you need to do what's best for her?"

Pressing Sam closer, Balashi spoke in his ear. "Sometimes children do not always know what is best for them. Amata has already lost her mother. She feared she'd also lose her father if I adopted you. But she and I talked last night. She truly does care for you as a brother. When she saw you were gone this morning, she realized how much she wants you as part of our family. It just took her a little longer to figure that out. Now, wash and get ready for bed." Balashi ruffled Sam's hair. "When we get back to Susa tomorrow, we have a lot of packing to do."

†††

Amata and Balashi tried to describe Babylon to Sam, but nothing prepared him for the sight of the majestic structures he saw two weeks later as he crossed the wide moat and entered Babylon's large city gates.

As they passed by a huge Babylonian ziggurat, Sam stopped in his tracks and let his mouth drop open. "What is that?" he asked, pointing at the huge rectangular-stepped tower.

"The building is called *Et-em-en-an-ki*," Balashi explained. "It means, *the temple connecting the sky and earth*. This magnificent temple is one of King Hammurabi's great achievements."

"It must be as tall as twenty houses, one stacked upon another." Sam leaned back as he tried to see the top.

"That is a good estimate, Sam. They say the temple stands approximately 200 cubits high. It contains seven levels, each smaller than the last. And, as you can see, an elegant staircase connects each floor."

Sam continued to stare as Balashi explained the structure.

"There are 600 rooms, each dedicated to a different god. All of the rooms are richly decorated with precious stones. Each room also has many statues. Hammurabi hired the best craftsmen to form gold and silver images of the gods and goddesses. Other statues he had carved out of wood from the cedars of Lebanon."

Sam let out a low whistle, still craning his neck to see the top. "Surely the gods must be pleased with such an enormous building, No wonder the Great Hammurabi has been able to live in peace!"

Amata tugged on Sam's robe, encouraging him to continue down the road as she assumed the role of tour guide. "Only a local maiden is allowed on the top floor of the temple," she said as they strode on. "And the top level has only one room. This room contains a bed and a solid gold table. It's said the god Marduk stays there each time he returns to Earth."

Sam looked ahead and then pointed to a large palace on the left. "Is that where the Great Hammurabi lives?"

"Yes." Balashi nodded. "And our new home is not far from it."

Turning down a hardened-dirt path, Balashi led them past a row of single-level mud brick homes. All had outdoor wash areas and ovens, but none had windows facing the street. The trio then turned down another path where Sam saw rows of two-story plastered and whitewashed mud brick dwellings.

Balashi stopped in front of one and threw his arm out to the side. "Welcome, my children. This is our new home."

CHAPTER 8

LURS

After their first month in Babylon, Sam began to feel at home. Amata continued her studies with a reading tutor in the mornings. In the afternoons, she worked with female servants who taught her skills in weaving and cooking. They had their evenings free for reading or play. Sam enjoyed his early morning rounds with Balashi, making house calls on important capital officials who had various ailments. In the afternoon, he and Balashi usually saw patients in the palace.

Summer gave way to autumn. Late one evening, he and Balashi were summoned to care for Hammurabi's son who complained of a stomachache. The boy had eaten an entire cake earlier that evening and only admitted it when Balashi insisted that the boy tell him everything he had eaten that day.

A week later, when Sam, Balashi, and Amata retired to the sitting room after a late dinner, Sam heard a knock at the door. Seconds later, a servant announced the arrival of two young soldiers who were asking to see the great asu.

"Yes," Balashi nodded to the servant. "Let them in."

The two men entered the sitting room, one leaning on the

other. Sam noticed something familiar about the injured soldier but couldn't figure out what it was.

"Please sir." The injured man looked at Balashi. "I have come all the way from Susa to see you. I was injured in a skirmish with nomads from the Zagros Mountains. I stayed in Susa to heal, but my injury only worsened. The asus in Susa told me I should come to see you when I returned to Babylon."

Balashi rose from his wicker chair. "Follow me," he told the two men. "And, Samsuluna, come with me also."

Leading the soldiers into one of the servant's quarters, Balashi pointed to the bed. "Lie down, please, and let me examine you."

The injured soldier removed a pouch from around his waist and placed it on a bamboo table next to the bed. After lying down, he lifted up his short, red tunic. "I was stabbed in the chest," the soldier explained, "and as you can see, it began to heal. Before long, however, it grew red and irritated and opened up again. Now it feels hot to the touch."

"Samsuluna," Balashi instructed, "wash the wound and treat it with aloe. I will return after I prepare a tumeric compress."

"Yes, sir." Sam scurried to the medicine room, retrieved the aloe, then filled a bowl with clean water. Returning to the room, he asked the young man, "So you recently fought in Susa?"

The soldier nodded, then winced as he tried to sit up.

Sam motioned for him to lie back down. "We recently moved here from Susa." Sam bathed the wound, then applied the thick liquid aloe.

"My battalion is stationed here in Babylon," the wounded man said, "but we received orders to assist the battalion in Susa. The Susa battalion had trouble rounding up some nomad bandits who were hiding in the foothills of the Zagros Mountains. Together, we tracked them to a local tavern in one of their villages. They put up a good fight, as you can see from my wound. My parents live in Susa, so I stayed behind to recover

while the rest of my battalion brought the prisoners back here to Babylon."

"Perhaps that's why you look familiar!" Sam shouted. "Do your parents own a bakery shop in Susa?"

"Yes, they do." A grin traced the soldier's face. "My brother Enlil told me that, if I saw you, I should say hello. You are young Sam, Enlil's friend, are you not?"

"Yes, I'm Sam." He nodded. "And you—you're Enlil's brother?" His heart inched to his throat. He hadn't said goodbye to Enlil before they moved to Babylon. He thought his friend was still mad at him for dumping him into the water. "Is Enlil still mad at me for flipping over his raft?"

"He told me about that." The soldier arched a brow. "Enlil says he isn't mad anymore, and that he misses you and Amata. He hopes you both come back soon to visit."

Balashi returned with the compress. "This must be changed every few hours," he said. Helping the soldier into a sitting position, he pressed the compress against the man's wound and secured it with strips of linen. "By the way, what is your name, young man?"

"He's Enlil's older brother," Sam blurted out.

Balashi's bushy brows squeezed together.

Sam lowered his gaze. "Sorry, sir."

Turning his head toward Balashi, the soldier said, "I am called Lurs, good doctor."

The other soldier, still standing in the corner, stepped closer. "Asu, will I be able to take my friend back to the palace barracks tonight?"

"No, not tonight." Balashi shook his head. "Since this compress needs to be changed every few hours, it would be best for him to spend the night here under our roof. I will send a messenger to the barracks tomorrow to let you know of his condition."

The other soldier nodded and left.

Balashi tightened the warp. "Now, how did you say you sustained this wound?"

"As I was telling young Sam here, my battalion was sent out from Babylon to help the Susa battalion capture raiding nomads living in the Zagros Mountains. I'm told those mountain men often raid sheep and cattle owned by the good people of Susa. Some even break into shops. They always run back to the foothills to hide. One evening, we discovered they were holed up in a local pub in a Zagros Mountain village. We surrounded the tavern and captured them, but they put up a good fight. My battalion brought the prisoners here to Babylon, while I stayed in Susa to heal. After a while, the Susa asus realized there was nothing more they could do for me, so they sent me back home. I was told to seek you out once I arrived."

"Balashi is the best asu in all of Babylon," Sam said with a nod of his head.

Lurs shifted his weight on the bed and grimaced. "Actually, I'm almost grateful for my wound. You see, three weeks ago, my wife gave birth to our first-born son here in Babylon. I now have a good excuse to stay home for a while as I recuperate." Lurs pointed to his pouch on the nearby table. "Before I forget, Sam, there's something for you in there."

Sam handed Lurs the pouch.

Lurs withdrew a small clay tablet and handed it to Sam. "Enlil wanted me to give you this message."

Sam glanced at it while Balashi helped Lurs lie down again.

With tablet in hand, Sam asked Balashi, "Is there anything else you need me to do here, sir?"

"No, that is all Sam. You may go."

Rushing out of the room, Sam found Amata working at her loom in the sitting area. Catching his breath, he thrust the tablet in front of her face. "Read this, Amata. It's from Enlil."

She set aside her shed stick and read the tablet aloud.

Sam. I overheard a conversation while delivering bread to the grog shop. Negrel plans to go to Babylon soon to form a new caravan headed for Tyre. I also found out that Negrel still has your jewels.

Amata handed the reddish-brown tablet back to Sam. "Is this the caravan driver you told me about? The one whose men beat you up, then left you for dead outside the tavern in Susa?"

The tablet trembled in Sam's hands as he recalled the burly man's greasy moustache and beard, his oversized hands, his ale-stenched breath. "Yes. That's the one."

Over the last month, Sam had told Amata about the jewels that his brother had stolen from their landlord. The only thing he hadn't told her was that his father was still alive.

The color drained from Amata's face. "Sam, you're not thinking of trying to get those jewels back, are you?"

CHAPTER 9

HAMMURABI'S CODE

A few weeks later, Captain Iridu, the captain of the Susa battalion, summoned Balashi to the palace guards' barracks where he was staying. Sam accompanied him.

Captain Iridu, like Lurs, had been injured while fighting the Zagros Mountain nomads. He helped bring the captured thieves to Babylon, in spite of breaking his arm during his battle with them. The physicians in Susa had bandaged the captain's arm, assuring him it would heal quickly. It hadn't.

"It's a good thing you called for me," Balashi said after examining the captain's arm. "Whoever tended your broken arm in Susa didn't splint it correctly. If you ever hope to wield a sword or dagger again, we need to re-break the arm and set it correctly."

The captain's nostrils flared. A wave of anger flooded his eyes. With his good arm, he fingered the dagger that hung from his side. "The doctor in Susa who tended my arm will certainly hear from me!"

Sam eyed the captain's dagger more closely. He noticed three round indentations in the hilt. "Captain, may I ask why you have empty spaces on your dagger?"

The captain's eyes softened. "My great-grandfather gave me this dagger shortly before he died." Captain Iridu withdrew the knife from its sheath. "He was a mighty warrior. His dagger's hilt used to contain three jewels, but they were stolen from me two years ago in Susa."

Staring at the empty places that once held jewels, the captain continued. "My men threw me a welcoming party when I first arrived in Susa. I knew many of them from my previous assignment in Ur. We had a little too much to drink that night, but somehow I managed to make it up to my room at the inn. I neglected to secure my door, however, and when I awoke the next morning, my dagger was gone. I found it later, outside in the rubbish heap, but the thief had removed the jewels." The captain paused and looked down at his misshapen arm. "By the gods, I swear, Susa has held nothing but bad luck for me ever since!"

Balashi turned to Sam. "Son, it looks as though my job here will take longer than I expected. We were supposed to see Lurs next at his home. Will you please let him know I will not be able to see him until later this afternoon?"

Sam bowed. "Yes sir." He maintained a respectful demeanor until he left the barracks.

Once outside, he raised thankful hands to the gods. He hadn't learned yet how to set bones. The thought of it made his stomach churn. He'd have to learn, eventually, but not today.

Lurs had stayed with Balashi for a few days, but was now finishing his recuperation at home with an occasional visit from the asu. Because of Lurs' new baby, Balashi sometimes sent Sam or Amata to check up on the family and to lend a hand. Sam looked forward to the visits. He enjoyed playing with the baby and hearing Lurs' stories about military life.

†††

"Sam, come in!" Lurs' wife greeted him when he arrived. "So good to see you. Is Balashi with you?"

"No, ma'am. He sent me ahead to let you know he will be detained until later this afternoon."

"Well then," she said as she escorted him into the living area. "We have a surprise for you. Look who just arrived from Susa!"

Behind Lurs' wife stood a bushy-haired boy.

"Enlil!" Sam shouted as he ran over and grasped his friend's shoulders. "It's so good to see you. What are you doing here?"

The boys sat down on mats near the eating table. Lurs' wife placed a bowl of pears in front of them.

Never one to refuse food, Sam plucked out a large one and bit into it. Juice formed around his lips.

"When my parents heard about Lurs' injury," Enlil said, "they sent me to help. Mother would have come herself, but my father can't manage the bakery shop without her."

"Neta," Enlil paused, "since the baby is sleeping now, would you mind if Sam and I went out? I'd like him to show me some of the city."

"That's fine, Enlil," Neta said. "Just be back before dinner."

"You know me," Enlil said, giving her one of his broad, toothy grins. "I'm never late for a meal!"

Sam led Enlil toward the palace compound to show him Hammurabi's five-cubit-high stone monument.

"So how is life in the big city?" Enlil asked Sam as they strode down several streets, then up a slight incline.

"It's very exciting." Sam said. "Balashi has taught me much about the healing arts. I've also learned to read and have even learned a little about politics and geography."

Finally reaching the palace compound, Sam pointed to the black stone pillar that loomed in front of them. "Here it is." Sam pointed to the giant tablet with Hammurabi's laws inscribed upon it. "I've been told that no other ruler has written down his laws for all to see, such as Hammurabi has done. Other rulers often change their decrees and judgments whenever they feel like it. On a whim, a ruler can deal out harsh punishment for one crime, but then give a light sentence to someone he favors. Here in Babylon, however, Hammurabi, his governors, and his judges must all provide the same penalties for the same crimes. They can't favor one person over another, for example, just because a criminal might be a good friend of the judge. See?"

Enlil nodded yes.

Sam pointed to one of the columns on the stele. "Read what it says here."

Enlil craned his neck upward and read aloud. "'I am the salvation-bearing shepherd whose staff is straight. My staff's good shadow spreads over my city so that the strong might not injure the weak, and to protect the widows and orphans.'"

Enlil met Sam's gaze. "So, King Hammurabi is not just a money-hungry ruler living up in his palace. This makes it sound like he really cares about the people."

Sam glanced at his crippled leg. "I always hated people in power. Especially my father." His voice lowered. "To me, people with power always represented pain and injustice." Then, thinking fondly of Balashi, he added, "I had no idea it could be any different."

Sam and Enlil continued to scan the tall black obelisk.

"Look at this law," Enlil said. "It talks about adoption."

Sam drew closer and read the lines Enlil had pointed out. "'If a man adopts a child as a son and rears him, this grown son cannot be demanded back again.'"

"And here's another." Enlil pointed to the next column. 'If an artisan has undertaken to rear a child and teaches him his craft, he cannot be demanded back.' Well, nothing there for you to worry about." Enlil quirked a grin. "Since both your parents are dead, there's no one to demand you back."

"Right." Sam wet his lips and then pulled them into a straight line.

Enlil continued to read out loud. "If anyone steals the minor son of another, he shall be put to death."

Sam's eyes widened. He pushed Enlil aside and moved closer to the black granite to read the line for himself.

If anyone steals the minor son of another, he shall be put to death.

He thought what this might mean for him. If court officials found out his father was still alive, could Balashi be put to death for adopting him without permission?

Angry shouts exploded in the next courtyard. Curious to find out what was going on, Sam strode through a stone archway and out into an open plaza.

Enlil followed.

About fifteen cubits away, a group of about twenty prisoners stood chained together in front of a raised platform. A tall, bearded man sat in a high-backed stone chair on a raised platform. With a crimson-colored robe draped around his shoulders, and a gold cone-shaped hat atop his head, he looked like an official you would not want to cross. A red-fringed canopy shaded him from the sun that blazed down on the prisoners standing in front of him.

Guards in red tunics surrounded the prisoners, occasionally poking them with their spear tips.

An angry mob stood behind the prisoners, shouting obscenities. Some in the crowd threw rotten melons and cabbage at the shackled captives.

The bearded man in the stone chair glared down at the prisoners and shouted. "You men of the Zagros Mountains have been charged with theft and causing bodily harm to soldiers of our great king, Hammurabi."

Sam wanted to get a better look at the prisoners. He squeezed his way through the sweaty-smelling mob until he made his way to the front. Spotting a familiar face among the prisoners, the air inside his lungs froze.

About six cubits in front of him stood his father. Instinctively, he patted his robe to make sure he still had his lucky dagger strapped to his side.

He did.

CHAPTER 10

SAM'S FATHER

Sam slipped back through the crowd to find Enlil.

"What's the matter?" Enlil said. "You look like you've seen a ghost!"

"You might say that," Sam licked his dry lips.

From the back of the mob, he could still hear the judge's strong clear voice. After reading a tablet in front of him, the judge called out. "I understand there are others here from Susa who have also brought charges against these men."

"Yes, I have other charges," a scratchy voice called out from the crowd. The scrawny figure of Zaidu, their family's creditor and landlord, wriggled out from the center of the mob and move toward the front.

"One of these men owed me the labor of his two sons for one year," Zaidu shook his upraised hand. "After only two months, one son got himself killed while watching my flocks, and the other ran away. I demand retribution!"

Sam wondered why Zaidu didn't say anything about the stolen jewels.

"Have the man responsible for these crimes brought before me," the judge demanded. Zaidu pointed out Sam's father. A guard unchained him from his fellow-prisoner, shoved him to the front of the stage, and pushed him into a kneeling position below the judge.

"What is your name, prisoner?" The judge leaned down.

"Dagon, sir." Sam's father didn't look up.

"And what do you say to these charges?"

"The charges are true," Dagon said. "I owe Zaidu money that I cannot repay."

The judge sat back in his stone chair. "If you cannot pay your debt, I sentence you to a year in prison here in Babylon." The judge gazed down at a scribe sitting at his feet. "Write this down."

The scribe carved marks onto a wet clay tablet as the judge continued.

"Any sheep, cattle, or other goods you have will be turned over to your creditor to help pay your debt. Once you have completed a year in prison, your debt will be forgiven. This case is now dismissed."

Sweat trickled down Sam's back. "Enlil, let's go down to the river. I need to think."

Sam took Enlil to one of his favorite spots along the Euphrates River near a stand of willow trees. The river flowed through the capital of Babylon and was busy at every point except for a section near these trees. Beneath the willows lay two large boulders. Sam and Enlil sat with their backs against the large rocks and skipped stones across the river's smooth surface.

"Enlil, I'm in a lot of trouble," Sam finally said. "I feel like I've made a mess of things. I don't know what to do."

"I'm listening," Enlil tossed a pebble into the water.

"You know the man we saw today? The one who owed the creditor money?" Sam continued to skip stones while leaning against the boulder.

"Yeah."

"He's my father."

Enlil turned toward Sam with wide eyes. "I thought your parents were both dead."

Sam rested his head in his hands. "I lied. And now my father will spend a year in prison because I ran away from our landlord. And that's not the worst of it." He lifted his head and glanced at Enlil. "What if my father finds out Balashi adopted me without him agreeing to it?"

"What?" Enlil's eyes widened even more.

A slight breeze rustled the willow branches.

Enlil stood and fisted his hands to his waist. "From what we read on Hammurabi's pillar today, I think Balashi could be killed for adopting you if the authorities ever found out."

A moan escaped from deep within Sam's chest as he nodded. "And then there are the jewels. The caravan driver stole them from me, but my brother originally stole them from our creditor. I would have used them to travel to Tyre if Negrel hadn't taken them from me."

"W-wait!" Enlil held up a hand and stepped closer to Sam. "Let me get this straight. You're not really an orphan, and you've been adopted without your father's consent. You ran away from your creditor, and now your father's going to prison."

Sam nodded.

Pulling in a breath, Enlil continued. "And if that weren't enough, the jewels stolen from you were actually stolen by your brother from someone else?"

"That about sums it up." Sam picked up a pebble next to him and threw it into the river.

Enlil whistled. "You're right. You are in a lot of trouble."

The next afternoon, as agreed, Sam met with Enlil again near the river. This time, however, he brought Amata with him.

"It's good to see you again, Enlil." Amata offered him a quick hug, then stepped back.

A toothy grin widened Enlil's face, but he offered Sam a raised brow as he gave his friend a sidelong glance. "I thought we were going to discuss certain problems today, Sam."

Sitting in the shade of the willows, Sam nodded. "We were. We are."

The other two joined him next to the boulders.

"You and Amata have been such good friends to me," Sam began. "I thought maybe the three of us could figure a way out of this mess."

Arranging her long green dress around her, Amata raised her chin to Sam. "Well, running away is not an option. You've already tried that, and we will not allow it to happen again."

Relaxing his shoulders, Sam allowed a faint smile to cross his lips.

"Let's tackle the adoption problem first," Enlil said. "What's the worst thing that could happen if you asked your father's permission to let Balashi legally adopt you?"

Sam pulled out clumps of grass from around his feet. "My father could say no. I'd have to go back to the Zagros Mountains and work for Zaidu for another eight months. After that, I'd have to go back and live with my father." Sam shuddered.

"That doesn't seem fair." Amata pursed her lips.

"No, but it is *just*," Enlil said. "And if you continue to pretend your father is dead, the truth will probably come out eventually. When it does, that will certainly make things bad for Balashi."

"Amata," Sam said. He swallowed, hoping to dislodge what felt like a chunk of dried bread caught in his throat. "You know I would never do anything to hurt you or Balashi. I must do what's right. I see that, now."

Amata turned her head away, stood up, and, after hiking up her gown, traipsed down to the river.

Sam stood to go after her, but Enlil grabbed his arm.

"Let her be for now," Enlil said. "I think she needs to be alone."

Sam sat and slumped against the boulder.

Scratching his bushy head of hair, Enlil turned to Sam. "That whole thing about having to work eight months for your landlord. Isn't that really your *father's* debt?"

"Yes," Sam nodded. "But, by law, my father can legally hire me out to pay off his debts."

"Yes," Enlil drawled out, "but what if you came into some money and were able to pay off that debt?"

Sam cocked his head. "Then I suppose I wouldn't have to work for Zaidu. But how could I—"

"Remember the jewels?" Enlil interrupted, his eyebrows shooting up.

"The jewels Negrel stole from me? What about them?"

Enlil tapped his chin. "I'm not quite sure, but I have a hunch that they might come in handy."

A splash came from near the river, followed by a scream.

Sam's heart clutched. *Amata!* He darted toward the water.

When he reached her side, he bit his tongue to keep from laughing. Glancing at the muddy river's edge, he saw Amata had taken three steps forward before falling into the water. He giggled as she flailed her arms in an effort to regain her balance. The more she tried to stand, the more she slipped, covering herself in more mud.

Reaching the river's edge, Enlil brought a hand to his mouth and laughed.

With wet goo plastering her face and arms, Amata shouted, "Well, don't just stand there. Get me out of here!"

CHAPTER 11

THE PROMOTION

$\mathcal{T}$he time for secrecy had come to an end. Sam told Balashi the truth about his father, the landlord, the caravan driver, and the jewels. The cloud that always seemed to float overhead disappeared. No matter the outcome, Sam knew he had the love and support of Balashi, Amata, and Enlil. With that, he could face whatever happened.

Balashi arranged for a meeting between Sam and his father. Dark rainclouds gathered as Sam entered the prison compound with Balashi. Guards guided them through musty stone corridors until they reached the section that housed Sam's father.

The stench of human sweat and waste assaulted Sam's senses, but it didn't weaken his resolve. He had to confront the man. When they reached his father's small cell, Sam peered through the bronze bars. In the dim light of the corridor's torches, he counted eight prisoners housed together in the dank, cold space.

The guard's large keys clanked as he unlocked the door and swung it open. The raggedly-clothed prisoners sat on the dirt floor, each with an arm shackled to one of the walls. Sam stepped inside, motioning for Balashi to wait outside the cell.

"Hello, Father," Sam began in a low voice.

Sam's father lifted his head, glanced at Sam, and growled.

"How dare you call me Father," he spat out. "You desert your dead brother, run away from your obligations, and get me thrown into prison. How *dare* you call me Father." Dagon turned away.

A rat scurried across Dagon's feet. He kicked at it but missed.

Sam grit his teeth. He guessed his father would blame him for everything. He guessed right. Throwing back his shoulders, Sam steeled himself against the accusations.

"Father," he began, "I'm sorry you went to prison because I ran away from Zaidu. I'll try to make that right. However, I've come to ask your permission on a very important matter." Sam paused and took a step back. "Since I left Zaidu, I've come under the care of an asu here in Babylon. He thought you were dead, so he took me in as an apprentice and then adopted me. Now that he knows you're alive, he'd like your permission to make the adoption legal."

Dagon, still sitting on the floor, slowly raised his head. He stared at Sam through a strand of his greasy black hair. A cruel smirk crept across his face. "I suppose you wish I *were* dead." Dagon cursed and spat. "Oh yes, dear son of mine—*only* son of mine. Then you'd be free of all you owe me." Dagon yanked back his shackled arm, then thrust it forward as if to hit Sam. The chain rattled as his blow fell short. Dagon's head drooped as he lowered his arm to his lap.

The torch in the prison hallway flickered, casting ghoulish shadows on the cell's walls. Once again, Dagon raised his head. Fixing his gaze on Sam, his face twisted into an ugly scowl. "And what's to become of *me* if I give this doctor permission to adopt you? Who will care for *me* in my old age?"

Shifting in his sandaled feet, Sam glanced at Balashi outside the cell. This was not going well.

"Of course," his father continued, "if this asu is a *rich* asu, I might reconsider." His father wet his lips with a blackened tongue. "Maybe this asu will pay for the privilege of adopting you." Dagon raised a brow. "I might let him adopt you if he's rich enough to cover my debt to Zaidu. And if he provides me with enough money to keep me comfortable the rest of my life. What do you think, Sam?" Dagon's mouth twisted again. "Does this doctor care for you that much?" He snickered. "I doubt it. What good are you? You're just a poor, stupid, crippled boy."

Sam's lower lip trembled. Anger and shame bit at his heart. He would never ask Balashi to pay his father for the *privilege* of adopting him. He'd rather go to prison himself. Why was his father so hateful? Sam recalled Balashi's words when he'd tried to run away. *Children do not have to deserve their parents' love.* That would never be true of him.

Earlier that day, Balashi had invited Lurs' family to join them for dinner. When Sam returned from visiting his father, the tantalizing smell of Eshe's slow-roasted mutton wafted in from the outside oven. His hunger roused, Sam scanned the cooking area for something to eat. Spying a stack of flatbread, he snagged a piece when Eshe's back was turned.

Chomping down the bread, Sam entered the house. Eshe had set the dining table with blue-colored wine chalices, copper plates, and eating utensils. Sam had never seen Balashi's fancy goblets. They usually used earthenware cups and plates. Puzzled, Sam searched for Balashi to ask him about it.

He found him in the sitting room, sipping a cup of tea. "Father," Sam asked as he approached. "Is there something special about dinner this evening?"

Balashi sighed and leaned back in his wooden, leather-cushioned chair. "Samsuluna, tonight I'm celebrating the gift of family and friends."

Family. The word rang hollow inside Sam's chest. How could he ever repay Balashi's kindness, or earn the right to be called his son?

††††

Lurs, Enlil, Neta, and the baby arrived by late afternoon. When Lurs entered, he immediately announced, "I have good news to share tonight."

"What is it?" Sam's previously somber mood brightened.

"Eshe has dinner ready," Balashi interrupted. "Let's all take a seat in the dining area."

As Balashi ushered everyone into the next room, Lurs wagged a finger at Sam. "Be patient, young Sam. First we eat. Then we talk."

"I can do both." Sam folded his legs beneath him and sat on a cushion next to Enlil.

"We know." Amata pinched a corner of her mouth and raised her eyes to the ceiling. "But it's not polite."

Ignoring her, Sam shot Enlil a sidelong glance and raised a brow. Maybe Enlil knew what was going on.

His friend simply shrugged.

Balashi and Lurs exchanged pleasantries about the weather and tidbits of news regarding the empire's possible expansion into Mari. Halfway through the meal, Neta put the baby down for the evening.

Once everyone had finished eating, Lurs stood and stretched. "Ah, that was a magnificent meal, Balashi. I suppose we should head home now."

Sam widened his eyes. "No, Lurs. You can't leave yet. You said you had news to share."

Lurs winked at Balashi and sat. "Oh, right. I did say something about an announcement, didn't I."

Shooting Sam a wry smile, Lurs sat and pulled out a small roll of papyrus from within his tunic. Placing it on the table next to his goblet, the young soldier leaned forward. "Captain Iridu of the Susa battalion is holding a banquet here in Babylon next week to celebrate new commissions. With southern Mesopotamia firmly under Hammurabi's control, Captain Iridu has been promoted to the position of commander. He plans to establish three new battalions—two here in Babylon and one in Susa. He's asked me to head up the new Susa battalion."

"Wait." Enlil pressed his palms on the table. "Don't *captains* lead battalions? Does that mean you're being promoted to ..." Enlil mouth fell open without finishing his thought.

Lurs interlaced his fingers, sat back, and smiled.

"To captain," Sam shouted out. "That's wonderful!" Sam attempted to let out a whistle between his fingers, but Amata grabbed his arm.

"Yes, it is wonderful." Lurs nodded in Sam's direction. "I'm proud to serve our Great King Hammurabi and to have the chance to lead a battalion."

Lur's wife patted his hand, a mix of pride and concern flooding her face. "Now that we are a family of three, I'm comforted to know Lurs will be close to home and not fighting somewhere on a battlefield. I never planned to marry a soldier, but I know the army is his passion. It will also be nice to move to Susa and be closer to Lurs' parents."

Sam glanced at Enlil. The scowl on his friend's face hinted Enlil didn't share his brother's enthusiasm.

Enlil worked his jaw and stared at his brother across the table. "You said you'd only be in the army for three years. After that, you promised Father you'd take over the family business."

Lurs' face darkened. Two stubborn lines formed between his brows. "Things have changed, Enlil. The family business is now your responsibility. I've discovered my destiny. It's my calling to serve in the army, not a bakery."

Enlil's flattened palms clenched into fists. "But what about—"

Before Enlil could finish, Lurs picked up the scroll he'd place next to his place and turned to Balashi. "Sir, Captain Iridu asked me to also invite you to the commissioning ceremony. Both Captain Iridu and I would be honored to have you and your family attend."

A banquet? Food? Entertainment? Sam's pulse raced.

"And, of course"—Lurs shifted his gaze to Enlil—"all of my family will be there. All except Mother and Father. They need to stay in Susa to run the bakery."

Enlil glanced away, a scowl still marring his brow.

Sam scratched his head. Why couldn't Enlil be happy for his brother? Then he recalled what Enlil shared that day on the raft. *Someday, I hope to work as a caravan driver.*

A sadness washed through Sam. It burned his insides. Lurs' plans would dash Enlil's hopes. Sam's sadness soon lifted, however, when an idea formed in his mind. A way to possibly solve the problem of the stolen jewels.

"Lurs," Sam leaned forward, "When my Babylonian tutor taught me about government, he said there's usually a change in city leadership when a new captain is assigned to an area. Will that be true in Susa when you move back there?"

"Yes, usually." Lurs said. "In my experience, before an outgoing battalion leader vacates his position, he usually appoints new city officials. He chooses men that will be loyal to the king, and who will help make the new captain's transition smooth. Why do you ask, Sam?"

"Oh, I'm just reviewing what I've learned about government and politics. I want to make sure I learned my lessons correctly."

Sam shot Amata a mischievous grin and winked.

He had a plan.

CHAPTER 12

THE PLAN

Late the next afternoon, after making house calls with Balashi, Sam sat cross-legged with Enlil and Lurs around their low eating table. While Neta put the baby down for a nap, Sam told Lurs about his father, and about Negrel and Zaidu. He then related his plan for getting back the stolen jewels.

"It's a crazy plan," Lurs said, "but it just might work."

Nodding, Enlil polished off the last date palm from the bowl in front of them. "That's what I said."

Lurs leaned toward Sam who sat across from him. "Let me get this straight. You want me to invite Negrel and Zaidu to the commissioning banquet. Are you sure they're still in Babylon? How will I find them? And, since I don't even know them, what reason will I give for inviting them?"

Enlil grabbed Lurs' arm. "That's easy. Sam and I have been watching Negrel and Zaidu in our free time. When Negrel's not preparing for his caravan drive to Tyre, he hangs out at the tavern near the caravansary. It's at the southern end of the city. His caravan leave in two weeks."

"And Zaidu is staying at the inn near the palace barracks," Sam added. "I've learned he's formed some money-making scheme with the innkeeper. He plans to stay in Babylon until the end of the month."

When Lurs explained the plan to his wife, she also agreed to help.

The next day, having told Balashi of their scheme, Sam, Enlil, and Neta baked a dozen loaves of bread. Later that evening, Sam, Enlil, and Lurs took the loaves to the pub frequented by Negrel.

While Lurs stayed outside, Enlil and Sam approached the tavern owner. Enlil told him his family sold bread to shops in Susa. "Our family is thinking of expanding our business to Babylon. We'd like to offer you twelve free loaves to serve your customers. If they like our bread, we could make your grog shop one of our first business partners when we open up a new shop here."

"Bread is bread." The plump owner shrugged and wiped his hands on his dingy apron. "Most of my customers drink so much that they can't tell a piece of bread from a piece of wood. But…." He went quiet for a moment, then shrugged again. "Free food is free food."

The owner handed the boys two knives. "I'm busy behind this counter refilling pitchers of ale. You two cut up the bread and hand out samples. We'll see what comes of it."

While the boys cut up a few loaves, Lurs entered.

Sam nodded in Negrel's direction.

Pulling up a stool, Lurs sat next to the huge man.

"I understand you're from Susa." Lurs waved down a helper to bring over a pitcher of ale.

"What of it?" Negrel growled.

"The name's Lurs." He slapped Negrel on the back as if they were old drinking buddies. "I've been appointed as captain for a new battalion in Susa."

Sam and Enlil passed out the bread samples to the customers, but Sam stayed within earshot of Negrel.

"I've asked around," Lurs continued. "Word is, you might be a good candidate for a leadership position when I move to Susa as the new battalion captain."

Negrel drained his cup, smacked it down on the wooden table, then sat up straight. "Well, I do have a good head for business. I also know a lot of important people in Susa. That's my main base of operations. Susa. Most say I have a persuasive way with people."

"I bet you do." Lurs eyed the men sitting near Negrel.

So did Sam. He recognized them as the thugs from Susa who'd beaten him up and stolen his jewels that night at the grog shop.

Withdrawing a roll of papyrus from inside his tunic, Lurs handed it to Negrel. "The outgoing captain of Susa, Captain Iridu, is hosting a banquet next week to celebrate his upcoming commission as a commander. I will also receive my captain's commission at that time. I'd like to invite you to the banquet. Attending could greatly enhance your chances of being chosen as one of the new leaders in Susa once I arrive."

Negrel grabbed the scroll, gazed at it, then studied Lurs. "What's the catch?"

Leaning back, Lurs raised his chin. "No catch. After the banquet, Iridu and I will discuss possible leadership candidates for Susa once I'm in charge of the new battalion. He, of course, has the final say. But because of the great things I've heard about you, I hope you can be one of the people we discuss."

Negrel tugged his scraggly beard and cleared his throat. "And what do I have to do to earn this glowing recommendation from you?"

Sam passed by, dropping slices of bread onto Negrel's table.

The caravan driver picked up a piece. He bit off a chunk and talked around it. "I'm sure having some kind of leadership position in Susa would be very beneficial to my caravan business, but I'm sure there must be a catch."

"Since you asked"—Lurs grasped Negrel's shoulder—"there is one thing that would greatly enhance your selection. You see, the captain's quite found of jewels. Especially emeralds, rubies, and diamonds. Actually, it's his wife. She's just crazy about them."

Negrel laughed and slid the invitation back to Lurs. "I knew there had to be a catch. What makes you think an honest businessman like me has access to such fine jewels?"

Lurs picked up the scroll and tapped it against Negrel's shoulder. "It so happens, the former captain's wife loves living in Susa. She doesn't want to move to Babylon, just because her husband has received a promotion. However, if Captain Iridu could find the right emerald, ruby, or diamond as a gift for her, I'm sure he'd be extremely grateful."

A slow smile crept across Negrel's face. "I just might be able to get my hands on one of them jewels." He scratched his bearded chin. "Which do you think she'd prefer?"

"Well, you see, that's the dilemma." Lurs shrugged. "Captain Iridu's wife is so moody. She changes her mind from day to day. If I were you, and if I had access to all three jewels, I'd bring all of them to the banquet. I can easily find out her mood during the banquet and let you know. Then, at the right time, you can present the perfect jewel to the captain. I'm sure that would earn you the attention and position you deserve."

When Sam and Enlil finished passing out the bread, they met at the back of the room.

"Whew." Enlil breathed out a sigh. "I'm glad that's done. I was afraid Negrel might recognize you and get suspicious."

"You worry too much, Enlil." Sam play-punched his friend's arm. "Even if he did recognize me, he'd have no reason to feel suspicious."

"Maybe so," Enlil said, "but before we go, let's ask for some water. I get thirsty when I'm nervous."

Sam nodded.

When Enlil asked the tavern keeper for water, the man set up two tin cups and grabbed a jug of water from the end of the counter. "Looks like my guests liked your bread," he said as he filled the cups. "Several asked for a whole loaf. Glad you brought me a dozen."

As Sam sipped his water, he continued to watch Negrel. The brute was now scanning the room. Sam turned to Enlil. "I'm going to move to the back of the room until Lurs is finished talking with Negrel."

Enlil nodded and poured himself another cup of water.

Retreating to the back corner, Sam noticed Negrel shift his attention to the front. Sam tapped the bronze dagger beneath his cloak.

Negrel cocked his head to the side and nudged one of the thugs sitting next to him. Leaning closer to the large man, Negrel whispered in his ear.

Moisture gathered on Sam's forehead. Had Negrel recognized Enlil from Susa? Even if he had, what difference did it make? Enlil's nervousness was rubbing off on him.

Negrel's goon stood and moved to the front counter.

Sweat tickled Sam's back. Negrel's ruffian said something to the owner who then handed him a pitcher of ale.

Sam wiped his palms on the sides of his tunic. Why did he feel so nervous? He didn't need a reason. His gut warned of danger. They had to get out. Now.

When Enlil turned to meet Sam's gaze, Sam motioned his head toward the door. Hopefully, Enlil would get the message and leave.

Instead, Enlil turned back to the counter. He drew circles on it with his fingertip. One of Enlil's nervous habits.

Negrel's thug picked up his pitcher of ale. Turning to leave, he bumped Enlil's cup, causing it to clatter to the ground.

"Oh, so sorry." Setting his pitcher of ale on the counter, the man retrieved Enlil's cup from the floor. "Here. Let me fill ya up again." He grabbed the water jug and refilled Enlil's cup. He then took his pitcher of ale to Negrel's table and sat across from the man.

Sam crept out from the shadows and motioned to Enlil, urging him to follow him outside.

Enlil finished his water, then existed the grog shop.

A few minutes later, Lurs joined the boys outside.

"That was close," Enlil said as they trekked back to Lurs' house. "I was afraid Negrel recognized me from Susa and sent his companion over to ask why I was in Babylon."

"And that make you nervous?" Lurs said.

Enlil kicked a rock down the road. "Negrel's seen me plenty of times at the grog shop in Susa, but I think he also knows I'm Sam's friend. Maybe he thought that if I was in Babylon, so was Sam. He might be afraid Sam would tell someone about him stealing his jewels."

Lurs ruffled Enlil's bushy brown hair. "You worry too much, brother. Everything went as planned. I've got him hooked. Negrel's going to bring the jewels to the banquet."

"I have to admit, Sam." Enlil kicked another a stone down the dirt path. "It was a pretty good plan. Now, for phase two. We jus…reel in…Nin..vu..wha." Enlil stopped mid-sentence. His arms twitched. His legs wobbled. "I feel…can't see..volley…"

"Enlil!" Sam shouted. "What's wrong?" Sam's heart hitched.

Lurs caught Enlil just before he fell to the ground.

CHAPTER 13

THE POISON

"What's wrong with Enlil?" Amata rushed to Enlil's side as Lurs carried his convulsing body into the spare bedroom.

"He was fine one moment." Sam tried to slow his panicked voice. "And then he started talking funny. He began to twitch all over."

Balashi scurried into the room carrying a tray of medicines. "Did Enlil have anything to eat or drink while you were out?" The asu leaned over Enlil's spasmodic frame as he lay on the bed.

"Just some water at the tavern." Sam trembled.

"Fetch some ground mustard and bits of black charcoal," Balashi instructed Sam. "And bring the pestle and mortar."

As if in a trance, Sam remained fixed, staring at Enlil's twitching body.

"Now!" Balashi barked.

Sam blinked, then ran from the room.

"And a fresh pitcher of water," Balashi shouted after him.

When Sam returned, Balashi was leaning close to Enlil's face. "Hmm. I detect a faint scent of honeydew melon." Grasping Enlil's fingers, he let out a sigh. "And his fingertips show a faint trace of something. Perhaps a green powder?"

Amata pressed a hand to her mouth. "Father, what is it? Is he going to die?"

Lurs stood by in silence.

Fighting back tears of fear, Sam moved closer to Balashi. "I've got the powdered mustard, charcoal, and water."

"Quickly, Sam," Balashi snapped. "Mix one part mustard to five parts of water."

Enlil thrashed about on the bed, shouting nonsensical words.

Sam stepped back and blinked several times as he took in the scene.

The asu held Enlil down and turned to Lurs. "Bring over the empty basin and towel from the corner table. Set the basin on the floor near Enlil's head."

When Sam finished mixing the mustard and water in a small bowl, he handed it to Balashi.

"Next," Balashi instructed Sam, "Crush the charcoal bits in the mortar bowl."

"Amata," Balashi shouted as he pinned Enlil's arms to his side. "Lift the boy's head."

Everyone obeyed.

"Hold down his arms," Balashi instructed Lurs. "I have to force him to drink the mustard mix." Balashi pressed the bowl to Enlil's lips and made him drink.

A minute later, Enlil sat up, leaned over, and retched into the basin on the floor.

"Sam," Balashi called out. "Mix one part charcoal powder with two parts of water."

Doing as he was told, Sam handed the concoction to the asu.

Repeating the process, Balashi pressed the charcoal cup to Enlil's lips and forced him to drink.

Nothing happened. Enlil flailed his limbs as if trying to break free of Lurs' grasp, and continued to say things that made no sense.

Sam wrung his hands. "It's all my fault," he cried out. "I never should have asked Enlil to go with us to the tavern." He moved to Enlil's bedside and grasped his twitching arm. "You've got to be okay, my friend. You've got to be okay."

"Samsuluna." Balashi, his voice now calm, rested a hand on Sam's head. "We have done what we can. You must let the poison work itself out of his system."

"But he can't die." Sam's nose tingled. "He just can't."

"Your panic will not help him heal faster." Balashi pried Sam's fingers from around Enlil's arm. "Take a stroll outside, son. Let me attend to the lad. I will call if anything changes."

Wiping his escaping tears on the sleeve of his brown tunic, Sam shuffled out.

About an hour later, Balashi joined Sam in the front of their house.

Sam lifted his eyes to the darkened sky, afraid to meet Balashi's gaze. "I never should have gone to the tavern. It was a stupid plan." Sam finally faced Balashi. "Is Enlil going to die?"

"No, son." Balashi draped an arm around Sam's shoulders. "The worst is over. The lad is resting quietly now. However, if we hadn't treated him right away ..." The asu's voice trailed off.

"What was wrong with him?" Sam swiped away a renegade tear.

Balashi pulled in a deep sigh. "I smelled the scent of honeydew melon on his breath. I also found traces of a green powder on his fingertips. You said he had a cup of water at the tavern, right?"

Sam nodded. "Yes, sir."

"I suspect someone poisoned his water with green lotus powder. As you may recall from our studies of poisons, lotus powder can be deadly. It causes a twitching of the limbs, blurred vision, and slurred speech. It can be fatal if not treated immediately."

Studying the ground, Sam lowered himself and sat. He leaned against their mud-brick home. "I think Negrel recognized Enlil from Susa and had one of his men poison him." Sam picked up a few pebbles from the ground near his feet and flung them into the inky night. "I don't belong here. I almost got my best friend killed by asking him to help me. And my real father. I hate him. I should just go to Tyre and find Uncle Zim."

Balashi gathered his robe around himself and sat next to Sam. Selecting a few stones from the surrounding dirt, he shifted them between his hands. "Finding your Uncle Zim will not solve your biggest problem, Samsuluna."

"And what is my biggest problem?" Sam wagged his head. "Is it finding a way to pay Zaidu back for the jewels? The ones I stole and then lost? Or is it that I lied to you about my father being dead and then tricked you into illegally adopting me? Or is it that I seem to hurt everyone who gets close to me— everyone I love?"

Images of his dead mother and brother floated across Sam's mind. An ache built up inside of him. Tears tumbled down his cheeks. He tucked his face into the folds of his robed arms, rested his head on his bent knees, and cried. Small gasps at first. Then, as waves of grief washed over him, his chest heaved with uncontrollable sobs and moans. Slowly, the tears lessened. After several more moments, he found it easier to breathe again.

As the quiet of the evening pressed in on them, Balashi leaned closer and whispered. "Forgiveness, Sam. That's your biggest problem. You need to learn how to forgive."

Sam glanced at Balashi, expecting him to say more.

He didn't.

The only sounds that reached Sam's ears were the chirping crickets and croaking frogs. "What do you mean?" Sam finally asked. Forgive who? Why? What are you talking about?"

"Forgive yourself. And your father."

Sam shook his head. "I've done too many bad things. I can't forgive myself. And I can never forgive my father. Because of him, my mother and brother are dead. Because of him I'll always walk with a limp. Because of him…" Sam's voice choked off. He buried his head in Balashi's robe. More tears trickled down his cheeks.

Balashi rocked him in a warm embrace. "Son, forgiveness does not mean you excuse someone's behavior or pretend that nothing happened. It means you deal with the pain and go on. You choose not to seek revenge."

Grasping Sam's shoulders, Balashi drew him back. "What do we always take with us when we visit the sick?"

Sam wiped his cheeks with the back of his hands and sniffled. "Our pouches of medicines and tools."

"And do we always have what we need?"

"Most of the time." Sam sniffed again. "But not always."

Balashi pressed his lips together for a moment. "Most of the time, parents carry a pouch filled with tools to care for their children—tools to love them, provide for them, protect them. Your father didn't have any of those tools in his pouch."

Sam tried to imagine his father carrying a pouch like the one Balashi carried when he visited the sick. In his mind, he opened his father's pouch. It was empty.

With trembling lips, Sam gazed at the stars. "Maybe if I'd been a better son. Maybe if I hadn't cried so much as a baby. Maybe then my father wouldn't have thrown me across the room." He stole a sideways glance at Balashi. "Maybe then, I wouldn't walk with this limp."

Like Sam, Balashi raised his eyes to the sky. "No, Sam. As I've told you before, children shouldn't have to earn their parents' love. Love should already be in a parent's pouch. Parents must teach their children right and wrong. But providing for, loving, and protecting your children—that should be unconditional."

Could Balashi's words be true? As if he'd swallowed a ball of fire, Sam's throat burned. He gulped in an effort to choke it down, but it wouldn't budge. He had no idea how long he sat there with Balashi, staring at the stars.

Finally, Sam wiped his damp face once more and spoke into the dark night. "My mother's pouch wasn't empty, but she died while Yasmah and I were working for Zaidu. I thought my brother's pouch was empty because he never stood up for me when my father beat me. But then, Yasmah died saving my life."

Sam turned and studied the faint outline of Balashi sitting next to him. "My father's pouch, however, was empty."

CHAPTER 14

THE JEWELED DAGGER

𝒥he night of the commissioning banquet finally arrived. Like the juggling entertainers who performed somersaults on the sides of the hall, Sam's stomach twisted, flipped, and whirled as he reviewed his plan. What if it failed? He wished Enlil were here. He had recovered from the poison, but Balashi said Enlil needed one more week of bedrest.

"Are you all right?" Amata grasped Sam's hand as they strode through the banquet hall to their assigned table.

He nodded as he met her gaze and allowed a smile to flit across his face. How beautiful she appeared in her new white gown. As the seamstress had suggested, she had clasped it together at one shoulder with a golden ring. He took note of the blue lapis lazuli necklace around her neck—the one she'd admired that day at the jewelry stall. Balashi must have gone back to purchase it for her.

Sam glanced around the huge hall. At the front, an upraised bank of tables faced the guests. Sitting tall, the former Susa captain, Iridu, sat next to his wife. With her hair neatly plaited atop her head, she wore a soft green gown that, like Amata, gathered at her shoulder.

On the other side of Iridu sat Lurs. How smart he looked

in his fine red soldier's tunic ribbed with silver stripes. Lurs' wife, Neta, sat next to him, her black hair elegantly coiffed and secured with a sparkling gold clasp.

Twisting in his chair to view those seated behind him, Sam spotted Zaidu at a table near the back. Earlier this week, as planned, Lurs had found a way to *accidentally* meet Zaidu and invite him to the banquet. Sam inhaled a shaky sigh. Their plan just *had* to work.

Once again facing forward, Sam noted the appetizers set out in front of him. The sight and scent of them made him salivate—legume soup, chate melon, figs, grapes, pears, plums, pomegranates, cheese, and a variety of breads. Biting into a piece of bread dotted with sesame seeds, Sam's mouth watered. He had never tasted bread with such finely-ground flour.

After he downed his soup and several handfuls of fruit, the servers brought out the main dishes. Plates heaped with pork, mutton, veal, duck, pigeon, and a variety of fish soon surrounded him. As he chewed his last bite of a date-sauced piece of pork, someone tapped shoulder.

"It's time," Lurs whispered in his ear.

Sam led Lurs toward the back of the hall where he'd seen Zaidu. "There," Sam said, pointing him out.

Nodding, Lurs placing a hand on Sam's shoulder. "Stay here where you won't be seen."

Like sentinels, two large lion statues adorned the rear of the hall. A winged bull guarded the middle. Behind the stone-carved statues, a yellow linen curtain covered the wall. Sam stepped behind the lion statue on the left. Every few seconds, he glanced out to watch their plan unfold.

Lurs approached Zaidu and whispered into his ear.

Smiling, Zaidu rose from his table and trailed Lurs to the back. Both of them slipped behind the yellow linen.

The curtain continued to hide Zaidu as Lurs crept out and

returned to Sam. "Now, for the second part of our plan," Lurs whispered.

Once again, Sam glanced out from behind the lion. Spotting Negrel, he pointed him out to Lurs. "Over there. Second table on the right, third seat from the end."

Rubbing his hands together, Lurs nodded. "I told Negrel to meet me by the winged bull when the meal was over. He should be heading over there any moment."

Just as Lurs predicted, Negrel left his table and tromped to the back of the room.

Lurs joined the caravan driver behind the winged bull statue.

From his hiding place behind the lion, Sam could see Lurs and Negrel. Hopefully, he was also close enough to hear what they said.

The large caravan driver tugged his beard and leaned close to Lurs. "So, which jewel does her highness favor tonight?"

"An emerald," Lurs said.

"Then an emerald gift it is." Negrel tugged his beard once more and tapped something beneath his mustard-colored tunic.

Zaidu crept out from behind the curtain and pressed a knife to Negrel's back.

Lurs slipped away as if he hadn't seen anything,

"Don't say a word, and don't turn around." Zaidu's voice sounded as scratchy as ever. "I hear you have my stolen jewels. I want them back."

"What are you talking about?" Negrel turned his head. Zaidu pressed the knife more firmly against his back.

"You know what I'm talking about," Zaidu said. "The jewels stolen from me by a crippled boy. And then stolen by you."

"I-I only have one of the jewels on me. The ruby," Negrel confessed. "Here. Take it." Negrel withdrew the ruby from a pouch beneath his tunic and slipped it to Zaidu.

"What? No diamond or emerald?" Zaidu growled. "I'm not

sure I believe you, but I'll take it. We will finish this conversation later."

An official at the front clapped his hands and called for everyone's attention. "As you know, tonight we honor the outgoing captain of the Susa battalion, Captain Iridu, and welcome him as the new commander of the Royal Battalions here in Babylon."

Applause rose from the audience as Sam returned to his seat next to Amata.

"Commander Iridu, would you like to say a few words?"

Commander Iridu, an impressive figure in his blue military tunic, pushed back his chair and stood. He nodded toward the guests. "I am honored to accept my new commission this evening. I am equally pleased to announce my replacement in Susa, the recently promoted Captain Lurs."

Lurs, having returned to his wife's side, stood and bowed.

Another round of applause filled the room.

The announcer raised his hands, motioning for silence. Turning to Commander Iridu, he bowed again. "There are several here who would like to show their gratitude for your years of service as captain of the Susa Battalion. I now call those people forward."

A line of about twenty-five people formed, each bearing some kind of gift. Commander Iridu and his wife received everyone individually, thanking each person as they presented their gift.

Negrel and Zaidu stood at the end of the line. Negrel tugged on his beard while he waited, and Zaidu shifted his weight from one foot to the other. Finally, Negrel stood in front of Commander Iridu and his wife. The large man bowed and handed the commander a leather pouch.

Commander Iridu, still seated behind the banquet table, withdrew an emerald from the bag and held it up.

The commander's wife leaned toward her husband for a closer look at the gem.

"You are from Susa, are you not?" the commander asked as he turned the emerald over in his palm.

Negrel cleared his throat. "Yes sir. I am a caravan driver from Susa. My name is Negrel. It would please me greatly if you and your wife accepted my gift."

Commander Iridu stood. "It shouldn't be difficult for me to accept your gift, Caravan Driver Negrel, since this emerald was mine to begin with."

"What?" Negrel stepped back.

Withdrawing the dagger from his side and placing the emerald into one of the indentations on his dagger's hilt, Commander Iridu raised the dagger for all to see. "Guards," he shouted. "Seize this man!"

The soldiers grabbed Negrel's arms, pressed them behind his back, and ushered him to the side to await further orders.

With eyes wide, Zaidu stepped back.

Lurs stood and whispered something to the commander.

With his dagger still upraised, the commander pointed to Zaidu. "Guards," he shouted. "Seize that man as well and bring him to me!"

The soldiers apprehended the squirming landlord and dragged him in front of Iridu.

"And whom do we have here?" The commander placed his dagger on the table and leaned across toward Zaidu. "Are you not also from Susa?"

Zaidu cowered. "I am a lowly landlord and creditor from the Zagros Mountains. I-I occasionally do business in Susa."

"And you were in line to also offer a token of gratitude?" The commander pulled his dark brows together.

"Ah, just this." Zaidu pulled out a bag from within his tunic and handed it to the commander.

Withdrawing a ruby from the pouch, Iridu held it up for all to see. "This is very interesting." The commander faced the crowd, and, raising his dagger again, fit the ruby into another indentation on his dagger's hilt. "Two men from Susa, each bearing a jewel that happens to fit into an empty space on my bronze dagger." He turned once more toward Zaidu. "You were an innkeeper in Susa two years ago, were you not?"

"Yes sir." Zaidu nodded.

"An innkeeper who, one night, took advantage of a new captain who had too much to drink. You stole these jewels from my dagger the first night I spent in Susa!"

"I was once an innkeeper in Susa," Zaidu squeaked out as he took a step back, "but now I am just a poor landlord from the Zagros Mountains. Those jewels were stolen from me by a crippled boy. His father is now in jail because he couldn't pay off the debts he owed me. I…I…" Zaidu, seeming to be at a loss for words, shriveled into himself as he covered his mouth with his hand.

After setting the jewels on the table, the commander returned his dagger to its sheath and folded his arms across his chest. "To quote Hammurabi's Code," the commander said, 'If anyone loses an article and finds it in the possession of another and it is proved to be stolen property, the thief shall be put to death.'"

Resting his palms on the table in front of him, Iridu glared at Zaidu. "If we search both you and the caravan driver, I believe we will find the third missing stone from my dagger. A diamond."

Commander Iridu turned to his guards. "Search them, then take them away. The courts will decide their fate."

CHAPTER 15

THE DECISION

After the guards dragged off Negrel and Zaidu, Amata stared at Sam. "What just happened?"

Sam explained the trap he and Lurs had set for the criminals, but was interrupted half-way through by oohs and ahs from the crowd. Glancing up, Sam discovered the source of the crowd's amazement. A man dressed in a silky blue robe led a large brown bear to the center of the stage. The evening's entertainment had begun.

After the blue-robed man waved a stick at the bear, the animal stood on his hind legs. The trainer shouted a command, and the bear, towering over the man as it stood upright, clapped his clawed paws together. The audience returned the applause. The trainer then commanded the bear to sit on a chair. As the bear sat, the chair broke beneath him. The crowd laughed. Both the trainer and the bear bowed their heads.

After the bear and trainer left the stage, three dark-skinned men with flutes and wicker baskets came out. Dressed in bulbous white breechcloths, the men blew a sweet tune on their double-piped flutes. As the music continued, large cobras emerged from their baskets. The snakes rose about eight cubits into the air. Their large-hooded heads swayed in time to the charmers' music.

Sam swayed too.

Next, a group of musicians carrying lyres and harps took the stage with several female dancers behind them. As the musicians plucked out a rhythmic melody, the women clapped small cymbals and rattled tambourines, all the while twirling and dancing in time with the music.

Amata tapped Sam. "Sam. Finish telling me about your plan. What did you and Lurs do?"

Pulling his gaze from the dancers, Sam turned to Amata. "When your father and I first visited Commander Iridu to examine his broken arm, I noticed he had three indentations on his dagger. It reminded me of the footprints you left in the mud that day we went down to the river. Remember?"

"How could I forget?" Amata's face pinched. "I ruined my favorite gown getting stuck in the mud that afternoon."

Sam grinned. "Well, like the muddy molds of your steps, the dagger's empty spaces told me something had been there that was now missing."

Amata shrugged her shoulders. "What does that have to do with the two men from Susa who were dragged away?"

"I'm getting to that." Sam raised a brow. "I also thought about the beautiful gown you bought, along with the shawl and the shoes—three beautiful things that went together. Then it clicked. The jewels were three beautiful stones that went together but had been stolen from their original setting."

Rounding her mouth as if to say, *Oh,* Amata nodded. "The commander's dagger."

The dancers finished, and the crowd applauded. Once the noise quieted down, Sam continued. "I figured Zaidu stole the jewels from the commander when they were both in Susa."

Amata pinched her lower lip between her teeth. "And your brother Yasmah later stole them from Zaidu. When you arrived in Susa, the caravan driver stole them from you."

"Yes." Sam nodded. "And according to Hammurabi's Code, a person cannot be convicted of theft unless the stolen property is found in his possession. So, Lurs and I got Zaidu and Negrel to each present at least one of the jewels to the commander."

"And now,"—the announcer came back to the stage—"we have one final announcement."

Sam faced forward.

The official raised a hand to quiet the crowd. "Our king and his court advisers have taken notice of an extremely gifted asu here in Babylon. Tonight I have the pleasure of announcing that the court has nominated this gifted asu for a year of study in Egypt."

Wide-eyed, Sam stared at Amata, then Balashi.

The official cleared his throat. "This prestigious award goes to Balashi ben Nahor."

Commander Iridu rose to his feet and applauded. Following him, Judge Mera and the priest of Nintu stood. Many around the room joined them in standing and giving a hearty applause. Sam recognized most as former patients of Balashi.

The official motioned Balashi to the front.

Mounting the stage's steps, Balashi bowed to Commander Iridu, Lurs, and the official.

The master of ceremonies unrolled a scroll and read it. "In acknowledgement of his healing skills and great thirst for knowledge, Balashi ben Nahor is hereby awarded a year of medical study in Egypt, all expenses to be paid by the court of Babylon. May he return with great knowledge that will benefit all of Babylonia's healers." The announcer handed the scroll to Balashi. "Would you mind saying a few words, Great Asu?"

Balashi bowed to the crowd as he accepted the award. "Many thanks to those who have bestowed this honor upon me," he began. "Many thanks to our great King Hammurabi for giving me this opportunity to visit Egypt and learn even more about the healing arts. I do not take this responsibility lightly. I will endeavor to learn all I can from the Egyptians. I promise to return and share that knowledge with all the great asus of our king's empire."

The next day, as the morning sun warmed his bedroom, Sam took time to ponder the events of the past few days. Before the banquet, Balashi told him he had gone to visit his father. His father had agreed to let Balashi adopt Sam in return for a sum that Balashi refused to disclose. Balashi also offered to help Sam find his uncle in Tyre, if that was what he still wanted.

Now, however, thanks to Balashi's commission to study medicine in Egypt, Sam had another option. Instead of going to Tyre, he could accompany Balashi and Amata to Egypt. There, Sam would also learn more about the healing arts. Sam promised to tell Balashi and Amata his decision first thing this morning.

Neither Balashi nor Amata spoke during breakfast. Amata opened her mouth several times as if to speak, but then closed it again.

Finally, Sam broke the silence. "So, I hear the weather is very nice in Egypt this time of year."

NOTES ON ANCIENT MEASUREMENTS

Did you know ancient civilizations like the Babylonians used measurements that are very similar to those we use today? In fact, it was the ancient Babylonians who came up with dividing an hour into sixty minutes, just like we use today!

Sixty appears to have been an important number in those days. The Mina was the standard weight measure in ancient Sumeria, and was about the same weight as one pound today. A Mina could be divided into sixty Shekels, and sixty Minas was equal to one Talent.

When it comes to distances, the oldest known long-distance linear measurement in the world is the Farsang. It was used in Babylon as far back as 4,000 years ago and equals about four miles. Another common measurement was the cubit, which was the length of a man's forearm. Although the cubit was used throughout much of the ancient world, it's exact length could vary significantly, since the length of every person's forearm is different. And while a cubit for a man typically averaged around eighteen inches, the cubit for a king was a bit longer than twenty inches.

In Babylonian measurement, a cubit was about eighteen inches, so the monument of Hammurabi's Code stood about seven and a half feet high.

THE ANCIENT ELEMENTS SERIES

Continue the adventures with Sam and Amata as they travel with Balashi to Egypt. What kind of trouble will Sam's impulsiveness get them into this time? What mysteries lie behind the gift of an alabaster jar and their discovery of a secret tomb? Find out in *The Alabaster Jar and the Hidden Tomb*, book two of Marie Sontag's Ancient Elements series. You can see a video trailer of *The Alabaster Jar & The Hidden Tomb* at:
https://youtu.be/qDAz4OQ8dvw

ABOUT THE AUTHOR

"Bringing the Past to Life—One Adventure at a Time," epitomizes the passion and writing career of Marie Sontag. She works to craft adventurous historical novels where middle-grade and young adult readers can walk alongside the characters, see what they see, feel what they feel, and experience how life in different times wasn't much different than in our own. Marie holds a BA in social science and an MA and Ph.D. in education. A teacher in California for over fifteen years, she now resides in Texas where she's often found playing princesses with her granddaughter, or super heroes with her grandson.

Visit Dr. Sontag online at:

www.mariesontag.com

Author's Notes

Dear Reader,

Thanks for joining me in this *Ancient Elements* adventure. Please consider having you or your parents leave a review on your favorite social medial platform or bookseller's website. If you enjoyed the story, tell a friend. Word of mouth is the best way to introduce stories to new readers. I'd love to hear from you. You can message me at mesontag@gmail.com, or post on my Facebook page at facebook.com/AuthorMarieSontag.

Dear Teacher,

Ready-made curriculum geared to national social studies and ELA standards for *The Bronze Dagger and The Stolen Jewels* can be found at https://www.mariesontag.com/resources-parents-teachers-homeschool-authors-students/. I love doing author visits at schools and connecting with students in person! To book an in-person or online author visit, contact me at mesontag@gmail.com.

Until our next adventure!

Marie Sontag

Made in the USA
Columbia, SC
19 August 2023

21825909R00064